Praise for L. V. Russell

"Blending gothic realism, lush prose, and a real talent for the creepy, L.V. Russel weaves a chilling love story that's certain to delight as much as it haunts."

— KATHERINE MACDONALD, *THE FAERIES OF THE UNDERWORLD*

"L.V. Russell's lyrical, descriptive prose shines... With a haunting atmosphere and an intriguing premise, this Gothic tale will capture your heart and keep it long after you've read the last page."

— CHESNEY INFALT, *ONCE UPON A TIME REIMAGINED SERIES*

"The Quiet Stillness of Empty Houses is a powerhouse of a novel that will live long in my memory. A gothic masterpiece that will shred every last nerve you possess and leave your hair standing on end. A beautiful, haunting piece of writing from L. V. Russell. Superb."

— STEPHEN BLACK, *THE KIRKWOOD SCOTT CHRONICLES*

The Quiet Stillness of Empty Houses

The Quiet Stillness of Empty Houses

L.V. RUSSELL

QUILL & CROW
PUBLISHING HOUSE

THE QUIET STILLNESS OF EMPTY HOUSES

BY L.V. RUSSELL

PUBLISHED BY QUILL & CROW PUBLISHING HOUSE

This book is a work of fiction. All incidents, dialogue, and characters, except for some well-known historical and public figures, are either products of the author's imagination or used in a fictitious manner. Any resemblance to actual persons, living or dead, or actual events is purely coincidental.

Copyright © 2023 by L.V. Russell

All rights reserved. Published in the United States by Quill & Crow Publishing House, Ohio. No portion of this book may be reproduced in any form without permission from the publisher, except as permitted by U.S. copyright law.

Cover Design by Fay Lane

Interior by Cassandra L. Thompson

Printed in the United States of America

ISBN: 978-1-958228-11-1

ISBN: 978-1-958228-10-4 (ebook)

Library of Congress Control Number: 2023903680

Publisher's Website: www.quillandcrowpublishinghouse.com

For my Mum & Dad, thank you for raising me in a house filled with ghosts

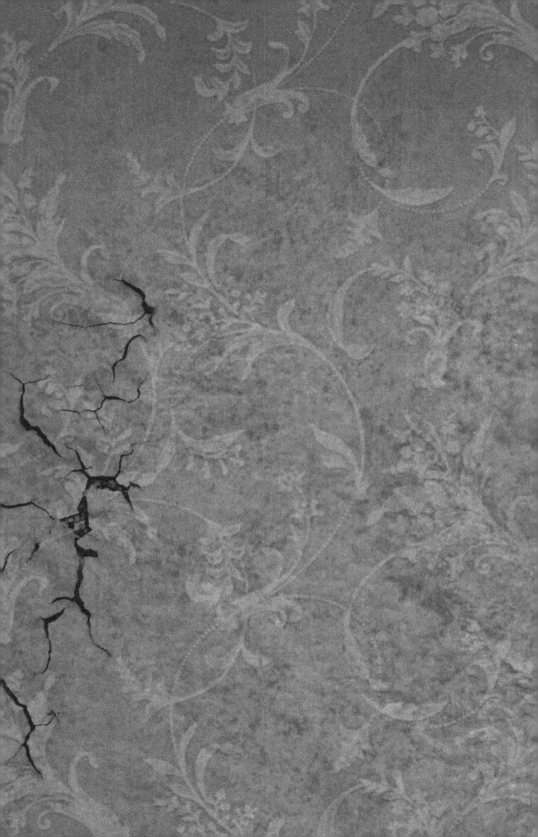

One

I am nobody, who are you?

Death was no stranger to Theodora Corvus. It had gathered at her cradle, whisper-soft and unseen, to take her mother's cooling hand. Upon the eve of her eighth midsummer, beneath the old oaks near the lake as the sun slipped behind the hills, Death also took her father's hand.

Age had not claimed him; it had only begun to show marks on his skin—a wrinkle at his eye, a thread of silver in his golden hair. It was a winter's cold that stilled the joy-filled heart of her father, an illness that had swept over all of them, even her grandmother. But where Theodora only suffered a minor fever, and her grandmother a sore throat and ill humors, it stole the life from the lord of Woodrow House. It took him in pieces, bled the color from his skin, the spark from his eye, the mirth from his lips, all so slowly. She had sat beside him, the dappled light sprinkling down from the green above, the trees watching over them, far older than the house. He had his blanket on his knees, his hand in hers and he did not say they were waiting for anything. But Theodora knew. So, as they waited, with the warmth of the summer air fading over them, the shadow of Woodrow at their backs, her father took a last lingering breath, and then took no more.

Theodora had watched him be lowered into the earth; her small hand clasped in the wrinkled folds of her grandmother's fingers. The old woman had turned to her, nose as sharp as the birds they were named for.

"Do not weep, child," Grandmother told her. "Save your tears for someone who will care to see them. Waste them not, for no good will they do you here."

So, Theodora swallowed her tears, and it was as though they never quite made it to her stomach, instead solidifying around her heart. She could feel it in her chest, the soft thudding of a grief-heavy organ. But she did not weep, and that made Grandmother very proud.

Her grandmother held her hand until long after the swarm of black-robed mourners had left and, with one passing glance at her son, tugged Theodora away. No tears stained her withered face.

I would care to see them, Grandmother.

Theodora was unused to grief, too young to miss her mother and too fearful to mourn her father. It sat there like a stone upon her chest. It allowed her to breathe, but only just, shallow and quick.

She shifted her body to allow for the weight, straightened her spine until her grief, that loss, became another part of her.

Woodrow House stood exactly a mile from the village, its crumbling white stone walls so covered in ivy, it looked as though the vines were stitching the cracks back together. It had belonged to the Corvus family for generations, and each generation had failed to maintain its sprawling corridors and pitched roofs, until it resembled nothing more than a damp husk. Parts of it had caved in completely, curling into itself like a giant spider.

Her father would have inherited it upon Grandmother's death. Theodora remembered the warmth of his hand in hers, his crooked smile as they both took in the decay and cobwebs. His voice had been warm and rich, like softened honey. "It should be condemned. Do not touch anything, Jackdora, I fear what horrible diseases linger in that floral wallpaper."

"Such nonsense," Grandmother had chided him. "One day, this will make a wonderful home for you and *Theodora*."

The emphasis on her name.

It did not go unmissed by Theodora. She did not dislike her given name, passed onto her by the mother she could not remember, but the name given to her by her father...that was special. That was hers alone.

Jackdora. Jackdaw. Named for the inquisitive and smallest member of the crow family.

Thomas Corvus tipped his head back to look up into the rafters, at the sunlight peeking through the rotten timbers. "Over my dead body, Mother."

And so, it had been. With her father far beneath the earth, Theodora stepped across the cracked flagstones of Woodrow House, the echoes of her father's sweet voice fading.

Winter took hold of Woodrow House like a disease. It settled into the eaves, crept through the pipes, ice forming as a ridged canker that even fireplace heat could not soften. Outside fared little better, the trees stark and brittle, the ground hidden beneath layers of white. Relentless mist coiled up from the lake, thicker than the cook's mushroom soup.

Theodora could see the lake from her bedroom window, its mist swirling around the brackish waters and dead-limbed trees bowing low at the water's edge. She saw the crows in the trees, and she would nod to them.

She saw the shadows of those once living, and they saw her too. She would nod to them like she did the birds.

They did not nod back.

She had spotted the black-eyed specters on her first night in Woodrow House, peering long into the mist to see if she could spot her father, or perhaps her mother.

"Not all the dead wish to wait, my dear," her grandmother had said, laying a withered hand over Theodora's shoulder. "There are those who should not linger, and yet still they do."

"What are they waiting for?"

A dry wheeze had rattled against the old bones of her grandmother's chest. "Salvation." The old woman coughed, a sharp sound that drew her hand up and painted it crimson.

"Father told you this house should be condemned," Theodora had said, turning away from the window.

"And yet you still ended up here too." Her smile had been red. "Your father refused to die in these halls and still he is beneath the earth. Death will come for us all in the end, darling. I would rather it be within this crumbling mausoleum."

Winter passed long and slow; it lingered at their hearth as an unwanted houseguest, drawing in the shadows, keeping in the cold. Theodora quickly grew accustomed to wearing multiple layers anytime she left her bedroom. She kept her stockings and mittens near the fireplace, so they were a welcome relief each morning. The few servants her grandmother kept would place warming pans in her bed, and she would fall asleep to the embers hissing around her toes.

Life fell into a slow and lonely pattern; one that Theodora found she did not mind. The stone against her chest remained, but its presence was one she had accepted. Her tear-hardened heart also became a comforting weight—a millstone carved by those she had lost.

She seldom saw her grandmother, whose bedroom stood at the far end of the house, up three flights of creaking stairs, and down a narrow and winding corridor. It was far enough away that Theodora could not hear her relentless coughing, the hiss and crackle of her determined lungs. Sometimes, the silence was worse.

On Sundays, she would call for Theodora, and they would sit and take tea. They would use the best tea service; the insides of the pot and cups stained a yellowish brown. She wondered if she too, was stained on the inside like everything around her, marred by time and neglect. Every treasure, every keepsake, took on an air of disuse. Everything once polished, buckling beneath the bowing weight of the house.

On those Sundays, with tea and cakes gone long dry, Theodora's grandmother would pet her head with a withered hand, comment on the lack of color in her cheeks, the limpness of her curls, and how she wished they were golden like her father's had been. She still refused to die, and Theodora gave her credit for that. She had little doubt Death had come to call on many occasions but, knowing her grandmother, she would have scoffed and sent him on his way.

She would not go until she was ready.

The rest of each week, Theodora took to exploring the ruins of the house, following the stoic servants through the corridors until they shooed her away. Rooms upon rooms had been left to rot, furnishings covered in once-white sheets; they lay over the collection of forgotten side tables and grand chairs like old gray ghosts, collecting dust and dead spiders.

She liked to wander down the cracked path at the back of the house to the mist covered lake. When the soft winter sun trickled from the clouds, no one else was around the too-still waters of the lake. She was not permitted to linger after dark; she was to stop searching the black-eyed echoes for traces of her father, for the face of a mother she did not know. They had not waited for her.

"Who are you?" Theodora called to the quiet waters, but the lake kept its secrets.

With the cold biting through her three pairs of stockings and good wool coat, Theodora turned away from the lake and walked back up the broken path to Woodrow House, whose shadow yawned open to swallow her. She took but a few steps upon the cracked stone path when, to her left, she spotted the wild flapping of a bird. A crow, it seemed, with one wing bent and broken. Theodora plucked it from the bushes, her fingers gentle, not caring that blood seeped over her velveteen mittens.

"I am a crow, also," Theodora said, tucking the bird close to her chest. "And, just like me, you do not belong here."

It was easy to creep back to her room without being seen; when no one was looking for you, you became invisible. With an old hatbox and a silk petticoat she had long outgrown, Theodora made a nest, and it was perfect. She settled the crow deep into the folds of her old undergarments, taking extra care not to jolt its wing.

The crow stared at her, black eyes not unlike those of the specters by the lake. It made no sound and ceased its flapping, and simply stared back at Theodora.

"I will name you Pallas and, together, we will fly away from this place. We will be friends, you and me. I am Theodora Corvus, but you can call me Jack."

Theodora slept soundly to the house's familiar creaking and groaning, its thumping pipes. She dreamt of black feathers and great wings, of being carried far from the doomed house and her grandmother's stubborn death rattle.

She woke with a smile, early winter sunlight breaking through the gap in the heavy curtains. Pallas's wings twitched as though itching to fly, though a milky film lay over its eyes.

With ever gentle hands, Theodora pulled the silk from its body, disturbing the fat little grubs harvesting its hollow chest.

It had not waited for her either.

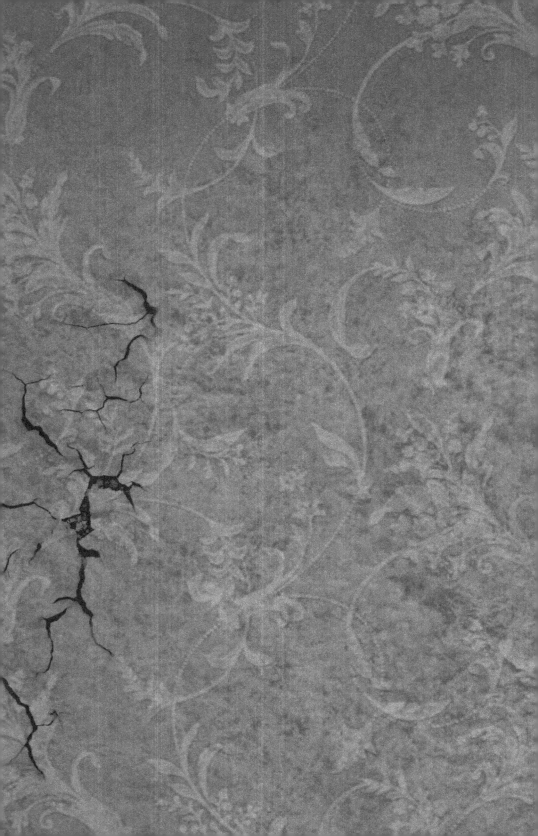

Two

Deep in earth, my love is dying

The years took more and more of Woodrow House; the old stone giving way to age and rot, the bones laid centuries before too brittle, too old, to hold it up. The years also took more and more of Theodora's grandmother. Her wrinkled skin grew thin like rice paper, spots of deep brown peppered her hands, and her fingers were twisted and stiff. The years had taken her eyes, the teeth from her mouth, the wit from her mind.

But the years passed and, still, death would not come for her.

Theodora often wondered whether her grandmother would outlive even her—as she had done the cook, the girl who swept the chimneys, and the postman. Theodora had taken up preparing meals, stoking the flames in the ancient cooker to roast meats and setting simple soups to simmer. She thought herself fortunate that her grandmother enjoyed her food bland, since she possessed little talent for cookery. She attempted to clean the fireplaces, but she feared the chimneys would catch alight with their collection of old bird nests and storm-blown branches, and that would be the end of Woodrow House.

"How are the children, darling?" her grandmother croaked from the bed she seldom left. Her old, blind eyes followed Theodora's hands as she set a steaming cup of tea upon her nightstand. The sharp green eyes of her youth had long faded, the milky film stretched over them masking the world from view. Yet still, with uncanny grace, Theodora's grandmother would turn her head and settle those unseeing eyes upon her. Theodora mused that perhaps her grandmother's hearing had sharpened where her eyes had dulled. The old bed stood mottled with woodworm, its coverlets faded, though the stitching was still fine, sewn by the grandmothers who had lived in the house in years past. Velvet curtains hung around the bed frame, pooling to the floor in a rich emerald puddle. Little decay had settled upon them, as though the house allowed her grandmother her privacy, this last fold of dignity.

"Agatha is learning her letters well, though Henry still insists on being troublesome. He let mice out in the schoolroom."

A sharp laugh burst from her grandmother's lips, followed by the old wheeze of her troubled lungs. "Boys will be boys, eh?"

Theodora brought her own tea to her lips, murmuring into the yellowy liquid. "Boys will be held accountable for their actions."

"I am blind, my darling, not deaf," Grandmother said, the laughter gone from her pale lips. "You are too like your father: he believed womenfolk should have their own voices. Oh, the things he would allow your mother to say!" She held a withered hand to her chest, as though she too had a stone there, a weight she had learned to curve her body around.

No tears. Never any tears.

"Tell me more about him, Grandmother." Hope, ever present, filled her voice. Theodora yearned for more stories of her father, more memories to fill the gaps in her own. They came seldom from her grandmother, fragments and little more. It seemed she hoarded them, as though in sharing she would lose hold of them and they would scatter to the winds.

The milky white of her grandmother's eyes searched for Theodora's deep brown ones. They roved over her body like she could see her —the darkness of her hair, the pallor of her skin, the thinness of her body.

Grandmother sniffed. "He would not have wanted you to become a governess."

The words struck Theodora's tear-heavy heart and danced off, like rain against a wax coat. "What would he have wanted for me?"

Her grandmother's filmy eyes stared through her, unblinking, unseeing. "Adventure, I would think. Something scandalous for a woman with your breeding."

"And who would take care of you, Grandmother, when I am on these adventures?" Theodora asked, her hand sliding along the rough covers to fold over her grandmother's, delicate fingers gentle upon skin so fine she feared it would tear beneath her touch.

Those age-stained hands gripped Theodora's, the bones creaking beneath. "Who indeed?"

Theodora could little imagine life away from Woodrow, to leave the heaviness of its dark and vacant rooms, to leave her grandmother to the shadows and solitude. Though she seemed not to mind it, the dark and the dust and the creeping rot, Theodora in all kindness was loath to leave her to bear it alone.

Kingsward Manor stood on the other side of the town, away from the mist, the lake, and the black-eye specters that watched and waited at the water's edge. It was a proud house of white stone and immaculate pillars. Its high windows were spotless, the wood around the frames smooth and oiled to perfection. No rot had set in, no long streams of ivy crawled up the sides to choke it. It was beautiful, classical, and elegant.

The rot was not within its walls.

The position of governess had come to Theodora quite unexpectedly, after the previous one had packed her things and, without a word to anyone, simply left. Her grandmother, with ever an ear for gossip despite her position as bedridden old crone, had sent Theodora with a letter of recommendation to take up the position. The Head of Staff took one look at the perfectly dressed Theodora, with her good breeding and good manners, and hired her on the spot.

It seemed no others had applied and, though that sat uncomfortably in the pit of her stomach, Theodora thought it bad form to question why no one else wanted the job. Since the new position was not too far away from Woodrow, Theodora had no need for accommodation. She took the carriage on days when it rained and enjoyed the long stretch of walking when the weather was fair. There was a comfort to Woodrow that Kingsward Manor lacked, and true as it was that the immaculate mansion was more weather tight, less decayed and crumbling, there seemed so little happiness beneath its roof, so little love.

The schoolroom at Kingsward Manor overlooked the well-manicured gardens. The windows were high, allowing light to flood the small room yet, despite the sunlight, the brightness, like the rest of the manor, lacked warmth in its perfection. The wallpaper was a soft yellow, expensive and fine, matching the threads of gold in the rugs underfoot. The school desks were polished, both without ink stains or carved letters, or any marks a child perhaps would make. Theodora remembered scoring her name in the soft wood of her own school desk, how she was reprimanded by her father for spelling it wrong.

"Agatha, I believe you have not been practicing your letters as I asked," Theodora began, leaning low over the desk where a pale-faced, pale-haired child sat. "They need to join seamlessly. Do it over, please."

The young girl looked up through long lashes, voice soft and pretty. "Yes, Miss Corvus."

"You are quiet this morning, Henry." Theodora turned to the young boy, just as pale as his sister. "Are there no mice to let loose in the classroom? No toads to slip into boots?"

The boy shook his head. "Father said a gentleman should not do such things."

"Oh? And what must a gentleman do?"

The boy thought for a moment, and Theodora contemplated how the children favored their mother in looks. "I think a gentleman should be allowed to do as he pleases, Miss Corvus."

Henry, it seemed, favored his father's temperaments. The boy was quick to anger and it was a strange, quiet sort of rage, one of plotting and scheming. He had a look about him, as though he were destined for either something great, or something awful, or both. He would make his mark on the world, Theodora surmised, as most spoilt men often did.

"Even if that brings humiliation to others? Or harm?" Theodora pressed, determined to instill some kindness and compassion into the strange little boy.

"What if they do not deserve my kindness, Miss Corvus?"

Theodora knelt beside the boy, skirts folding around her. "Does not every living thing deserve kindness, Henry? It is not simply a gift you bestow on those you deem worthy of it."

Henry was silent a moment, bright blue eyes fixed on hers. Then he glanced toward his sister and his lip curled. "With respect, Miss Corvus, I disagree."

When lessons ended and the children were finishing their supper, Theodora retreated to the small parlor set aside for her. It was a room for her to read and enjoy a cup of tea while still within earshot of the children. The room, though small, was pretty, its delicate wallpaper painted with lavender stems. It fitted a comfortable armchair, a side table, and even its own tiny fireplace. The window overlooked the lower parts of the garden, where Theodora would often see Lady Kingsward tending her roses, face pale and sad.

Theodora never saw the woman smile—not at her or her own children. Her face remained melancholy and wan, as though all life had bled from it. Theodora wondered what her own mother would have felt about her, if she had lived. If she would seek solace within the thorny tendrils of her garden like Lady Kingsward, able to snip away the rot to allow more life to bloom.

Her father had laughed, loudly and frequently, and she could not imagine him in the arms of someone who found no joy in life. But, when asked what her mother had been like, the laughter had stopped and, though he had tried very hard to swallow his tears, he had never been much good at it.

Lady Kingsward seemed to move with a strange soft grace, the hem of her exquisite gown always muddied by recent rain. Yet when the towering form of her husband loomed nearby, she stood straight, chin tilted up, the sadness within her eyes replaced with something Theodora had no name for.

A tap at the door broke Theodora's gaze from the gardens. She looked up to see Flora, one of the maids, hovering at the doorway. Her freckled hands twisted in the strings of her pinny, soft green eyes not quite meeting Theodora's. "Pardon the interruption, Miss Corvus. His lordship is asking for you."

They shared a look, then, one of knowing and understanding and quiet dread. For Flora, it was also one of pity.

"Did his lordship say a reason?" Of course, he had not; of the few times he had called for Theodora, never once was a reason given. She knew that the old lord often struck his staff, as quick to temper as his son. It was the kind of secret that everyone knew and everyone kept and no one ever shared. The only telling of it was the steady changing of staff, there was always someone new, replacing someone who may have been a friend, a familiar face, never to be seen again.

"I can mind the children, Miss Corvus, while you're gone."

"Thank you, Flora." Theodora smoothed the skirts of her stiff gown and checked her mouth for cake crumbs. "Help yourself to the peppermint tea, it would be a shame for it to go to waste."

~

Lord Kingsward's study was in the middle of the labyrinthine walls of the library. Books towered up the oak shelves, spines thick and pristine as though they had never been opened, to preserve their value. Once touched, one's worth decreased.

The study boasted no windows; the strange room lit only by the candlelight. The shadows in the corners remained black as ink, as though solid.

Theodora waited, perched upon one of the stiff-back chairs. She had been in the study a handful of times, and he had loomed over her, tall and thin, his hands curling over the armrests.

He would ask about her lessons—whether his son had a thirst for knowledge, whether his daughter could keep a fine conversation. It would not be long before each child was sent their separate ways. Henry would follow the path of his father and grandfathers. He would learn to be a lord, be taught law and literature and how to take everything he was owed simply because he could. It would be finishing school for Agatha, where she would learn to be pretty and perfect and quiet—a breeding doll for another lord who was owed one.

Lord Kingsward did not stand over her that afternoon, did not curl his long, long fingers over the edges of her armrests, did not breathe the scent of good whiskey and pipe smoke into her face. He sat behind his desk, pen in hand, as he finished signing a neat pile of letters. He had not looked up as Theodora had entered the room, simply nodded to the empty space opposite him and carried on working.

"The children will be missing me, my lord," Theodora spoke into the quiet, words soft against the scratching of the pen nib.

"Yes." Lord Kingsward placed the pen back into its holder, blowing gently on the glistening black ink. "Yes, I suppose they will."

"May I ask the reason for you calling me up here?"

Lord Kingsward looked up, silent for a moment. "Because I wished it so, Miss Corvus."

He stood, unfastening the fine cufflinks at his wrists before placing them beside the stack of letters. The soles of his well-polished boots tapped across the floor with deliberate slowness, four paces and he stood behind her. The door clicked shut and the lock turned.

Desolation—that look she had no name for—it was desolation, and Theodora learned it within that windowless room surrounded by books no one had read. It caved her body inward, and it left her hollow.

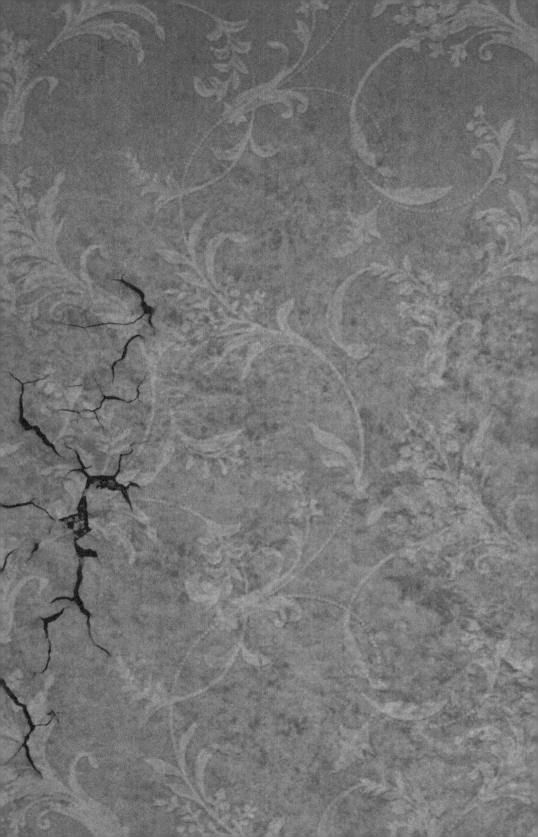

Three

I am fearless and therefore powerful

The dismissal did not come until the following month, weeks after the bruises had slipped from her wrists. Henry had set his eyes upon them first, the dark splotches of skin not quite hidden by long sleeves.

The boy furrowed his brow, as though concerned, and shook his head of pale curls with a tut upon his lips. "Carelessness, Miss Corvus," he said.

Theodora tugged at the sleeves of her gown, the marred skin upon her arms a deep yellow, rather than the vivid purple they had been. "Indeed, Henry. The grounds are slippery this time of year, I urge the both of you to mind your steps."

"It is careless, Miss Corvus," the boy continued, nose scrunched, "to leave a mark where one can see them. It is most vulgar, do you not think so, Agatha?"

The young girl said nothing, eyes darting back to the poem she was writing, her letters neat and small.

"I asked you a question and you will answer me." Henry reached out to pinch his sister's arms, fingers quick.

"I shall tell!" the girl hissed, forcing her arm away. She tugged the hemline of her dress up over her knees, past the pretty bows of her white stockings. "I shall, Henry, and then papa will beat you too."

Theodora could see the scratches upon Agatha, the red lines gouged out against pale skin, and turned to the boy, fury upon her tongue. "Did you hurt your sister, Henry?"

The boy tilted his chin, a smirk at his lips. "Only when needed, Miss Corvus."

"You will do no such thing again—do you hear me?" Her voice was firm, unwavering as she stared down at the insolent little lord.

"Will you tell Father?"

"And your mother, Henry. What would she think? You will not raise your hand to Agatha again, do you understand me?"

The boy stood, his small, childish fists curled at his sides. "I will not take demands from some dissolute whore—"

Theodora could never recall the back of her hand striking the boy, but the crack of his head against the flagstones—that sound, she would take to her grave.

It should have filled her with relief when the boy's sobs began, when he sat up and screeched at her. But for a moment...for a little longer than a moment, she wished he had remained silent.

So, the dismissal came, a quiet parting of awful, shared secrets.

Theodora's grandmother supplied little sympathy, lamenting how it would be difficult to find another placement in such an establishment as Kingsward House. She expressed even less sympathy for the boy, saying that, if it were permitted to strike young lords more often, the world would be quite a different place.

Theodora was left to fear what would happen to Agatha; was she to become as wraith-like as her mother? The thought sat heavy upon her tear-weighted heart, and she found herself keeping the girl in her prayers at night. For she could do no more for her than hope—hope that, despite the odds, despite the shadows already clinging to her, she would find love.

She spared little time on her own soul, simply tucking the fear and the grief into the little pocket of herself where she kept such things. She locked it tight and fastened the stays of her corset more firmly, in case the bulge of feelings was ever revealed to anyone else.

Since her grandmother loathed idle fingers, Theodora found herself put to work around Woodrow House. She minded little, the aches in her bones from sweeping and dusting and mopping settling over the aches of that dark little room. Her broken nails were chipped from the tiles over the fireplace. The bruises upon her legs from tumbling down the rotting stairwell at the back of the house. She ached because of hard work and nothing else.

She could not help but wonder that, if Woodrow House would not take her grandmother, it would take her instead.

When night fell and the house settled, its old bones shifting back into place, Theodora would stand and watch from her bedroom window. Spiderweb cracks spread along a few of the panes, the wood holding them in place blackened and brittle. It would no longer open, though it let in enough of a draft that it mattered little. It allowed a fair amount of light into her room, to settle upon the peeling yellow wallpaper, the old floorboards, and faded rugs. It lay upon her soft as butter and caught the whirl of dust motes that danced on the constant breeze.

In summer, she could barely make out the dark waters of the lake, the late sunshine revealing nothing but a few stoic crows waiting in the trees. It was in winter, with the branches stripped stark, that Theodora could see the black-eyed specters that watched her with such silence.

Once, she had left her bedroom to walk to the edge of the lake, to where the water lapped at the bank, black and cold. She had been able to see them so clearly, the paleness, the absence of color.

"Why do you watch me?" she had asked, voice echoing across the lake like a stone over water. "Grandmother says you seek salvation. Is it me that you seek? Can I help you?"

They had turned, a softness of wind, black eyes staring and staring and staring.

And then they had smiled, and Theodora had fled.

Each night, as the house began its slumber, Theodora would stand at her window, hand against the locked box within her chest, ensuring not even a spark of fear slipped out. With her chin held high, she stared out at the veil of ghosts, matching each and every one of their wide-mouthed grins with her own.

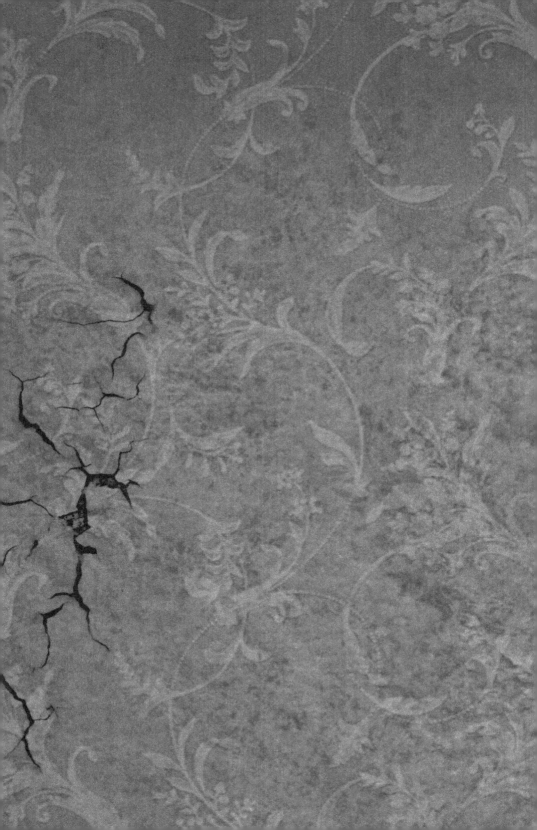

Four

I am no bird

Look here, darling!" the words rasped from Grandmother's thin lips, reaching across her faded bedspread to pass a yellowing letter to Theodora. There was a stack of them piled high upon her nightstand, some tea-stained and ripped. Some so old the paper had begun to curl and blacken. Woodrow left nothing untouched by its slow decay, it slipped across anything that lay still for too long. "It appears news of your indiscretion has not yet reached past Northton."

Theodora unfolded the letter, noting the broken seal. "They asked for me personally?"

"I have been putting out enquiries for a while now, dearest. Lest you find you are not so suited to where you found yourself."

"You have not left this room for many years, Grandmother. Who could you possibly—"

Grandmother waved off her words with a sniff. "I have means, the maid, I cannot ever recall her name, knows how to read and read she does. I have eyes that are not my own, and you would do well to acknowledge that. I know all the secrets beneath this roof, without having to leave my room."

"Do you have the servants spy on me, Grandmother?" Theodora asked, a wry smile at her lips.

"What other uses do they have?" she answered, wrinkled fingers running along the frayed edges of her bedcovers. "There is little use in dusting, when this house is little more than dust."

"I mind little helping here, Grandmother, it is no burden."

"You are not a serving girl, Theodora."

"But I am your granddaughter, your only living relative. That must mean something, surely?"

"There was little for you here before." Her grandmother swept out a hand, gesturing to the whole house, and quite possibly to the county beyond. "And even less since you struck that awful boy."

"It is a long way to go; I will be very far away from you." Theodora took in the address, written in faded ink. She read the slanted words, the handwriting neat, small, and unknown to her.

Crooked hands clasped her own, holding so tightly that, for a moment, Theodora feared they would snap around hers. "Adventure, darling. Adventure."

"Yet still a governess, Grandmother." A dry smile lifted the edges of Theodora's mouth, one that her grandmother echoed.

"Your father would have liked it less that you remain here, than to see you as a governess."

A briny droplet seeped from the corner of grandmother's cloudy eye, sinking deep into the folds of her skin. She did not seem to notice, and Theodora thought it most unkind to reveal it to her.

I care to see them, Grandmother.

A single tear for a son long buried.

Theodora took in the crumbling walls around her, the blackness of mold creeping over the walls like ink, the cracks in the window panes. Death would not claim her within its decomposing husk. Her father had wanted more for her. Adventure and romance, like the life he had lived.

"I could seek lodgings for you close by, Grandmother?"

"The dust of this house has settled in my bones, girl," came the rasping reply. "It has hardened them. My lungs contain the iron from the window frames, my heart the fire from the hearth. I am as much a part of this house as I am myself. It will not let me go."

"Then I will find more help—"

Another wave of her hand, dismissive. "The young maid will do. What is the skittish creature called, Amelie?"

"Annabel, Grandmother." The maid was one of the few remaining staff, shy and aloof, she had barely exchanged a few words with Theodora. She knew that was what her grandmother liked about her; the cleaning didn't matter, as long as one was quiet and fed her secrets and gossip.

"She will do. And I will tell her to send note when I do at last depart this world."

The thought of her taking her last breaths alone, in a room that stole the person she once was piece by piece, horrified Theodora. "I would be at your side, Grandmother!"

"Why? My passing will not be made easier with you looming over me, and I cannot see how it would bring comfort to you."

"Would you wait for me?"

Grandmother turned her blind eyes to the window, although the lake could not be seen from her bedroom. She looked out, with a gaze that no longer saw the world around her, but perhaps was not unseeing to the world beyond.

"I will not."

Grandmother did not leave her room to bid Theodora farewell, but had gifted her some very fine suitcases. The insides were pink silk, the leather a rich brown. Golden clasps held everything tight, and Theodora marveled at how lovely they were, strong enough to keep all manner of things locked away and secret.

With her dresses and petticoats folded carefully inside and her wash bag tightly secured with her favorite soap, Theodora stepped into the waiting carriage and rode away from Woodrow House. No one from the scant household stepped outside to wave her off, it was but her and the carriage and driver. It was a lonely farewell, but Theodora was used to being lonely; it brought a strange sense of comfort—a familiarity that nestled amongst the melancholy of leaving.

Woodrow slipped from view, crooked eaves disappearing beneath the tangle of woodland that had been left to grow wild. The winter-stripped boughs were still, all in darkness save for the ever-present ivy that snaked around them, that carpeted the ground, that hid the stone and the bones of all that had come before.

Past the lake they rode, and Theodora lifted a hand in farewell, peering through the thick mist to watch the black-eyed specters watch her leave.

They stood silent; the grins from their faces gone.

Theodora had never been to the north of the country—in fairness she had seldom strayed north of the small town she had been born in. Though north she would go, for hours and days until she arrived at the rolling heathlands that surrounded Broken Oak Manor. She was to care for a young girl of eight, the daughter of Lord and Lady Thorne. For friendship, the letter had stated, as well as for lessons.

Her gloved fingers folded and unfolded that letter, the edges torn, the expensive paper stained. It was an invitation for a new life, far from crumbling houses and untouched libraries.

The ride was long and lonesome, the driver silent and sullen, and the whip in his hand cruel. Darkness bled through the velvet curtains, wrapping around the single scrollwork lantern swaying back and forth above Theodora's head. Not that she minded the dark, for awful, awful things could happen beneath the sunlit sky, beneath the light of a hundred lanterns. Evil did not always seek solace in the shadows.

A picnic had been packed for her, corned beef sandwiches on thick cut bread, green apples and three hard boiled eggs. A piece of leftover sponge cake had been wrapped with care in a piece of oilcloth, the cream slightly curdled. Nestled among the food was a bottle of lemonade and a flask of tea. She picked at her offerings, enjoying that they looked as if they had all been packed with care—as if someone within the sloping walls of Woodrow had given her more than a second thought.

She dozed, hands folded in her lap, letter still beneath the silk of her gloves, as the world passed her by. Forests of old with their slumbering oaks slowly thinned to soft rolling hills lit only by the pale moon. Rivers widened and thinned, forking into streams that splashed the carriage wheels. They passed a few others, the lanterns of passing coaches lighting up as they clacked on by. The world slipped by in a soft quiet blur, with the beat of hooves and the turn of wheels, the odd slap of the whip.

Soon enough, the hills stretched into heathland, the heather soft and quiet beneath the dark cloak of winter. The road dipped and curved, as though cut from the earth with no thought to those who traveled it.

They reached the small inn where they would rest long after the sun had slipped below the horizon. The night was a solid blanket around them, unlit by stars, darkened by bruise-like clouds that hung heavy over everything,

The shabby building stood alone on the roadside, it was enough to rest the horses, feed the driver and allow Theodora a lukewarm bath and a soft bed. The driver had merely grunted down at her, not offering to take her hand as she clambered from the carriage. The landlady, she found, was nice enough, all rosy cheeks and bright smiles. It was enough kindness for Theodora, who was unused to such things; it warmed her through and kept her warm as they set out once more the next morning.

The hours passed in comfortable boredom, and Theodora was happy in her own company. The passing of the landscape was a novelty; the world rushed by, far larger than she could have ever imagined. She still kept the letter between her fingers, held tight in fear of losing it and being sent away. Sent home, where her grandmother would scold her carelessness and deem her as much of a disappointment as her father had been.

Theodora woke when her head struck the sidings, the letter floating to the floor. Darkness peered back from the window, as thick as good ink. The lone candle in the lantern flickered once and went out. The darkness from outside seeped around Theodora, settling over her shoulders like a cape without warmth.

"Are we lost, sir?" Theodora called to the driver, fumbling forward to press against the opposite side of the carriage. "Should we not stop?"

But the carriage continued, heedless. A small cry of alarm escaped Theodora as she was unseated, the carriage wheels hitting a ditch with an almighty snap.

The carriage rolled with the scream of horses, their brays sharp and sudden before being cut short. Her body slammed against the polished wood of the sidings. Over she went, breath knocked from her lungs, delicate skin cut by shards of glass from the window. Water poured in, cold and black, and still Theodora went over and over like beaten laundry.

It was an awful fear, to be trapped and drowning but, with some mercy and thanks to the blow to her head, Theodora sank into darkness and feared no more.

The world was quiet and soft when she came back to herself—almost as though she were back and safe in her father's embrace. But the scent of pipe-smoke and ink was absent, in its place the tang of dirty water and river weeds.

She lay against the embankment, legs half in the water, muddied gown tight around her body. Cold, so very cold, but seemingly uninjured. The night lay thick and heavy, the black starless. Theodora could see neither light from the lanterns, nor hear horses or coachmen.

"Help me?" The words slipped from her mouth near soundless, a question she found no answer to. "Please. Help me."

Within the tangle of night, Theodora dragged herself to her feet and climbed away from the rush of the river. Blindly, she tore through thicket and spindle-thin trees, hands stretched before her to feel through the darkness. On she stumbled, prayers at her lips until at last the dance of candlelight broke the velvet veil of night.

Lanterns flickered in welcome on either side of the manor's grand door, breaking through the pitch. It was a lighthouse in a storm, a salvation. Like a lost ship finding its way, Theodora fell upon Broken Oak Manor, bruised and beaten, but whole.

No tears.

No one would care to see them.

The house stood dark save for the soft glow of the lanterns flanking the doorway. With the gentle light, Theodora could see it was a grand house indeed, tall and solid, the stone gray. Great turrets spread on either side, curling around and up, the windows small and dark. Balconies and verandas broke from the walls, moonlight dusting the edges of the black railings. The unlit windows were criss-crossed with more black iron, and they towered over her, those windows, thin as narrowed eyes.

No one had been sent to greet her and, though Theodora would have greatly liked a friendly face, she was somewhat thankful that she would not be seen in her soaked gown and muddied stockings. Seeing nowhere else she could go, she walked up to the looming wooden door. Her silk-clad hand turned the handle, the door swinging upon heavy hinges onto a shadowed hallway.

Cringing at her muddied boots, Theodora stepped into Broken Oak Manor and straight into the path of a passing servant.

"Mother bless my soul!" The woman held one hand to her chest, the other reaching toward Theodora. "Lord have mercy, girl! What business have you scaring good folk?"

"I meant no harm, ma'am," Theodora said, wishing she could have made a better first impression. Her grandmother would be horrified. "I became quite lost on my way here, you see...my carriage overturned. I am the new governess, you should be expecting me? Theodora Corvus?"

The woman pursed her thin lips, dark eyes taking in every inch of Theodora's soaked and muddied state. She stood tall, her frame slightly bent, like an insect. A watery smile trickled at the edges of her mouth as she held out a hand. Theodora took the woman's thin fingers and bobbed a curtsy.

"The new governess, you say?" The woman nodded, smiling down at her hand within Theodora's. "Ottoline will be most thrilled."

"I am afraid my belongings were lost," Theodora said, following the housekeeper into the grand hallway. Carved pillars stood proud, spiraling up from the polished floors like stalagmites. "Is there someone who could check on the coachman? I could see so very little in the dark."

The housekeeper looked beyond Theodora, past the doorway, into the night. "Let us hope he has fared better than you, girl."

The insides of Broken Oak Manor yawned open to a twin staircase, dark stained wood beautifully sculpted with vines and leaves and intricate knots. The floor beneath her dirty feet shone, and the rugs were spotless. Unlike the crumbling splendor of her home, Broken Oak Manor bore no scars, no festering wounds. Unlike the cold perfection of Kingsward Manor, Broken Oak seemed to breathe warmth from its walls.

"You will find no one else at this hour." The housekeeper walked ahead, not waiting for Theodora to follow, her voice echoing behind her. "You will have to get used to the dark; his lordship is affected by the most terrible headaches."

"I am used to the dark, ma'am, that will not be a bother."

"I care not if it would be, girl," the housekeeper replied, tone soft and dismissive. "We no longer hold many staff here—it is but me, his Lordship, and Lady Ottoline. Where did you say you were sent from?"

"I didn't." Theodora quickened her pace, ensuring she kept up. "I am from Woodrow House, that is my family home. I was last in employment at Kingsward Manor."

"I see."

"You have heard of it?"

The housekeeper turned briefly, sharp gaze flicking to Theodora. "I have heard of both."

Theodora followed around the winding corridors of Broken Oak, the hallways narrow and dimly lit. The rugs beneath their feet kept their steps soundless, the darkness ahead banished only by the candle the housekeeper held before her.

Theodora took in the many paintings they passed, hung within gilded frames upon the wood-paneled walls. Many were landscapes, paintings of the heathlands surrounding the manor, a few were of the house itself. Those depictions revealed the sheer size of Broken Oak, different canvases showing different views, different towers, balconies, greenhouses.

"May I ask where Lady Thorne is?"

The housekeeper stopped at a door on the third floor, a small room tucked deep beneath the eaves of the house, high above the cavernous hallway beneath. "Milady is taking in the air at the seaside for her health. I believe she will be gone for some time. This will be your room; the fireplace will be lit if needed and should never be done by yourself—"

"I am most competent in lighting—"

"I did not question your ability or lack thereof, girl. You are not to touch the fireplaces. You are not to touch the candles. Those are the rules and, if they will be a problem for you to follow, I can show you the way out."

Theodora took in her small bedroom—the neatly tucked bed,

the desk and the chair. She turned to the window, small as it was, and saw by the moonlight that it looked out upon a lilypond shrouded in mist. Nothing stared back at her, nothing waited.

"I understand the rules, Ma'am. I feel I shall be very happy here."

The housekeeper nodded, thin lips curling ever so slightly at the edges into what Theodora believed was a smile. "You are to come down at six to greet Ottoline and begin her lessons. Do not be late." She gave another nod, then hesitated. "If you are to stay here, you are to call me Ms. Rivers."

Without another word, the woman left, closing the door behind her. The fire had at least been lit, its flames warm and welcoming and, upon the small side table, a single candle burned.

The bed was hard, and the blankets scratchy, but they were warm and clean and, for that, she was thankful. There was a small freedom to her placement at Broken Oak Manor, away from the guardianship of her grandmother, far from the shadow of Kingsward. Her room, though small and dark, overlooked the gardens that stood still and calm beneath the winter moon. Beneath the moonlight, she could see the sweeping lawns, the mature trees in the distance, the dark bricks of a walled garden.

Within the house, under the beams, the walls of Broken Oak neither groaned nor ached nor shifted beneath the constant weight of decay.

It was a good place, Theodora thought, a good place.

And for that, she was thankful.

The morning followed a restful sleep; the fire, though burning low, clung to the warmth of its dying embers. The candle at her bedside remained lit, its little flame breaking up the thick veil of darkness.

Theodora slipped from her room, careful not to wake anyone still sleeping. Down the unlit hallway she went, fingers running along the smooth walls. She remembered the way, too used to roaming the corridors of sprawling mansions to find herself lost in one. Silence was her only company, and it made her halt to rest her palm upon the wall. It remained still; she could not feel it breathe.

It was an odd thing, to have such an unmoving house with nothing to say.

"What secrets are you hiding?" Theodora whispered, tracing a hand over the paneling. "I promise not to tell a soul."

The house did not whisper back; it did not creak or groan or rumble. But perhaps, Theodora thought with a glance back into the shadows, perhaps the house was listening.

More light filled the kitchen, a large room with hooks for the copper pans and hooks for the herbs and hooks for the sausages, fat and pink. The fireplace crackled with life, flames licking the wood and spitting embers onto the red-tiled floor. A pot of real loose tea sat upon the table with two fine cups and saucers beside it.

"I find tea is the best way to start a day," Ms. Rivers said, making no sound upon the tiles as she walked in. She turned to the clock on the mantle, then back to Theodora. "You are five minutes early."

"I thought it best to be prompt on my first day."

"You'll get no thanks for it."

Theodora straightened her skirts and her back. "When will Miss Ottoline be down?"

"Shortly."

"And Lord Thorne?"

The housekeeper looked up, up at the kitchen ceiling as though she could see the rooms above. "His Lordship likes the dark and the quiet. You will do well to remember that, girl."

"Miss Corvus," Theodora said, meeting the housekeeper's gaze and keeping it. "If I am to remain here, you will call me Miss Corvus."

"Where else would you go, Miss Corvus?" The housekeeper gave her a thin-lipped smile. "Your tea is growing cold."

Theodora waited beside the hearth, near the fire, to warm the chill that had set into her bones. As soaked as she was when she had arrived, it would surprise her little if she fell ill. The fire blazed whole and hearty, but it seemed just as Woodrow House had claimed parts of her grandmother, it had laid claim to Theodora's bones and set them to ice.

Ottoline slipped into the kitchen at precisely half past six. She wore a smile that matched her pretty, frilled dress, innocent and lovely. Her fair hair lay in two plaits that hung over her shoulders, finished with cream linen bows. The girl owned a cherubic quality—her cheeks full, rosebud lips pink, freckles like stars. Her eyes, however, though a pleasant blue, lacked the warmth of the rest of her.

Theodora knew the look in her eyes, for it was the same that gazed back in the mirror. She took in the girl's hands, small and pale, hovering near her chest, where perhaps some secrets were kept tucked away and hidden.

"You must be Ottoline," said Theodora, bending low. "I am Miss Corvus, I do hope that we will become very good friends indeed."

The girl stood a moment, her head tilting up to peer at the ceiling to the rooms far above her. Then, without a sound, she stepped into Theodora's arms and held her tight.

The day bloomed cold but clear, the sky losing its slate gray blanket to reveal the soft blue below. The early morning mist recoiled from the pond's edges, its water clear and full of large fishes of the brightest orange. It was at the edge of the pond, alongside the tall blades of grass, the reeds, and the late blooming flowers that Theodora thought it best to sit with Ottoline so they could get better acquainted.

The house sat behind them with rays of watery sunlight bathing the stone in gentle light. The windows, however, were dark. It watched from its place on the gentle sloping hill, with those black, unblinking windows, in silence.

"I have asked Ms. Rivers to meet with your father today, Otto-line. I understand your mother is away?"

The girl fussed with the laces on her shoes before smoothing the folds in the blanket they sat upon. "Mother is taking in the air at the seaside, for her health, I am told. I have never been, Miss Corvus, have you?"

"To the seaside? I am afraid to say that I have not, but perhaps, when summer comes around and if your father permits it, we can go together."

A smile bloomed at the edges of Ottoline's lips. "We could build sandcastles and have ice cream and ride the donkeys down the promenade."

"We could go for a paddle and jump the waves," Theodora said, clasping Ottoline's small hand.

"I have heard that there is a carousel with dozens of golden horses that spin around and around and around. I would so love to go on one."

"We will write it all down, Ottoline, all these wishes, and pop them in a box for when the summer comes. Every time you do well in your lessons with me, you can write a wish, and I will do my best to help them come true."

Her eyes lit up, ever hopeful. "I would like that very much, Miss Corvus."

"Perhaps your father would like to come too? And your mother."

The smile slipped, and Ottoline turned to the unlit windows, looking toward whatever looked out upon them. "Perhaps."

Theodora followed the girl's gaze, eyes settling upon a watcher in one of the dark windows. It was taller than Ms. Rivers and straight-backed. Then, the curtain fell once again in place, and the watcher watched no more.

❧

The afternoon was given to Ottoline for reading and quiet play and meant that Theodora also had that time to herself, to enjoy as she saw fit. She had plans to meet with Lord Thorne to discuss which areas of Ottoline's education he would like her to focus upon.

It had been clear, even when first speaking with Ottoline, that she was intelligent and possessed a thirst for knowledge that almost outdid her own. But it was also clear that the girl was lonely, and Theodora vowed to herself that, not only would she be a good teacher, but also a good friend.

She waited in the sitting room alongside the kitchen. It was a pleasant space, kept for receiving visitors and keeping them comfortable until they were invited into the larger, more formal rooms deeper in the house. A small fire burned in the grate and a few candles in polished silver holders worked together to banish some of the darkness to the corners of the room.

The clock upon the mantle ticked by and still she waited. She knew little about Lord Cassias Thorne. She knew that he was the only son of the late Lord Thorne who, if she recalled correctly, was the cousin of the twelfth Earl of Shrewshire. Her grandmother had insisted that Theodora learn all about high society, but she always had trouble remembering her earls from her barons.

Grandmother had married the fourth son of an earl, a lowly lord of little consequence but in possession of a rather large house. Her son, to her eternal disappointment, had wed for love.

There was a lot to be said about lords and ladies in their grand houses with no one to share them with. Theodora wondered whether they all went a bit mad in the end, becoming part of the fixings as time plodded by, gaining a sort of immortality as their houses absorbed them.

The door clicked and Theodora stood, hands smoothing down the wrinkles in her skirt, still damp from her time sitting near the pond. She slipped into a curtsy, head bobbing low, but it was not Lord Thorne who graced the doorway.

Ms. Rivers peered into the room, one hand remaining upon the door handle. "His Lordship is plagued by one of his headaches and so will not be seeing you today, Miss Corvus." The housekeeper did not wait for a reply, thin lips pursed and pinched as she relayed her message and turned to leave.

"Perhaps tomorrow then?"

"How should I know?"

Theodora forced a smile. "I would be most grateful if you could pass on my wish to speak to Lord Thorne regarding his daughter. Never before have I been in a placement where I have not met my charge's guardians."

The housekeeper sniffed, taking in the slightly damp and rumbled appearance of Theodora. "Been in many placements then, have you?"

"Only the one."

"So I heard." Ms. Rivers took one of the candles from the sideboard and blew it out. "I will pass your wishes on, Miss Corvus. Enjoy the rest of your afternoon."

With the afternoon looming before her, Theodora took it upon herself to explore more of Broken Oak Manor—to wander its dark hallways and rooms. Not minding, Theodora climbed to the floor above hers, where many more of the servants would have slept had the house kept any. The floorboards beneath her remained sound, sturdy, and did not creak and groan like she was accustomed to. There was an empty echo to her footsteps, a loneliness to her walking.

Thin windows to her side allowed what was left of the daylight to seep in, catching the dust motes waltzing in the air before her. The cold, forgotten lanterns above were woven over by spiderwebs, the metal beneath dull from disuse. She turned a corner, revealing another set of stairs and, at the top, a door.

Ever curious, Theodora walked on, and the quiet of the house seeped around her—like a breath held.

"Come," it seemed to say, *"come see my secrets."*

Another step, her hand against the wall to feel for the beat of the house. The stone was cold and, when she scratched at it, hairline cracks spread like veins in the plaster. She stepped closer, the scent of cobweb and a strange sweetness seemed to emanate from beyond the door. Wiping the dust upon her skirts, Theodora reached for the door handle, the brass knob polished and unblemished, and turned it.

It did not give.

She tried again, unsure if age and lack of use had lodged it. Her curiosity ignited, she rattled the door in its frame, yet it refused to yield. Theodora felt it then—a shift in the air, the echo of empty footfalls. The sun had slipped away without her noticing, leaving her to face the dark corridor she had wandered down with the locked door and its brass handle at her back.

"Who are you?" she said into the shadow, and the shadow curled a small cold hand around hers.

"It is Ottoline, Miss Corvus. This is the attic; we do not use it anymore, and it is cold and damp. Come play with me instead."

So, Theodora returned down the unlit passageways, the stairs, and away from the old part of the house that no one used or visited and had left to slowly rot. She turned back just the once, wondering why, if no one came by the old attic, the door handle was polished quite so perfectly.

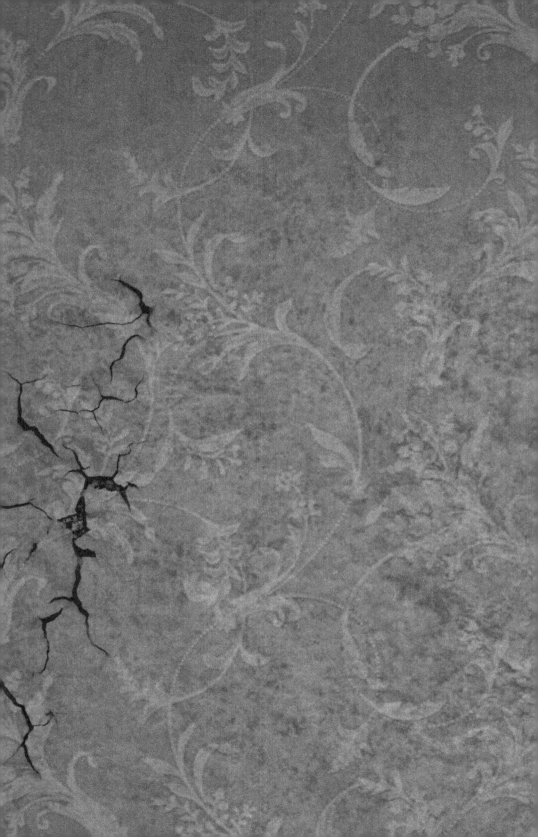

Five

In the night, in the dark

The evening drew in dark and cold, clouds gathering in a moody sky. Theodora watched from her small window as the sunset bowed beyond the horizon, dragging the clear winter day with it. Rain spattered the glass, fat droplets that turned to hail as quickly as it had come.

She had settled Ottoline into bed and tucked her in tight, leaving her to sleep with the soft candlelight dancing over the walls. The lessons that afternoon, after the house grew dark, had been taken in the sitting room, beside the fire. It was a comfortable place, a better place to get to know the young girl. The housekeeper minded not, and sat by the fire with her cup of steaming tea and crochet. Theodora and Ottoline sat on the rug, legs stretched out, so close that their skirts were touching.

"Tell me more about yourself, Ottoline," Theodora had asked, pointing her cold toes toward the fireplace.

Ottoline pulled her legs up, chin resting on her knees. "I thought you were to teach me, Miss Corvus."

"Ah." Theodora had smiled. "But first you must teach me. What are your favorite things?"

"I like the garden, Miss Corvus," Ottoline answered, eyes closing as if to remember. "I like playing around by the roses, skipping over the wall, hiding from Papa. I enjoyed making herbal tea from the lemon balm in the garden...but I no longer like the taste of it."

"I made tea once from leaves in our garden when I was young," Theodora had replied, recalling the grit from the soil, the mulchy taste of old vegetation. "It did not occur to me that there were some leaves that made good tea, and others that did not."

Ottoline's lips had twitched into a near smile, her blue eyes brightening. "A bitter tea is hard to forget."

"Quite so, Ottoline." Theodora reached across the rug to take Ottoline's hand. "Is there anything you would like to know about me?"

The young girl had looked up, all soft eyes and pale hair. "Will you stay, Miss Corvus?"

And Theodora had held tight the small hand of Ottoline Thorne and answered as honestly as she could. "For as long as I am able."

Ms. Rivers had been in to light her fire and the few candles she was permitted to banish at least a little of the darkness. She had spoken only a few words to Theodora before leaving her to her thoughts in the dim little room.

Theodora did not mind the quiet or the loneliness; the servants at Woodrow House had seldom spoken to her, and her grandmother was not much for idle chatter. She remembered, though, her father's kind words, how they had come quick and soft from his mouth. Always unbidden, those words, almost subconscious—as though it had been the most natural thing in all the world for him to remind Theodora how much she was cherished.

She placed a hand against the weight in her chest, the feelings inside a little too full, a little too ready to spill over. She swallowed once, and again, and any tears that may have begun to seep at the corners of her eyes went away.

At her little desk, Theodora took pen to paper.

Dearest Grandmother,

I have arrived at Broken Oak safely, though my journey was far from peaceful. I am afraid to say our carriage overturned and I had to finish the last few miles on foot! You should have seen the state of me, turning up at the front door looking half drowned. I truly thought I would die from shame. It saddens me to write that the beautiful set of silk-lined cases have been quite lost, along with everything that wasn't already on my back.

The housekeeper, Ms. Rivers, has taken good care of me and, although she is a little stern, I do think we will become friends in no time. I have myself a small room that overlooks the lilypond, which is nothing like the lake at Woodrow. From what I can see, there is not a soul lingering amongst the lily pads.

I have met the darling Ottoline, who I am to teach. She is a wonderful young lady, Grandmother, so kind, if a little sad. I am hoping that, in the coming weeks, I will change that.
I have yet to meet Lord Thorne, as he has taken ill, but I shall pen another letter to you when, finally, I get to meet him.

I hope this letter finds you well, and that you and Woodrow are still standing strong without me by your side. I love and miss you.

Your doting granddaughter,
Theodora

Theodora sealed the envelope and set the letter aside to be sent out with the post the next day. She missed her grandmother—missed the rattle of her bones, the rasp of her voice, her harsh determination to ignore death's waiting hand. But she would find comfort in her words; that she knew, and that would be enough.

Hoping to see Lord Thorne the following day, Theodora settled into bed, listening for the sounds of the house settling down. There was nothing save for the soft fall of rain against the window.

~

The darkness was a solid thing when she awoke, stirred from slumber by the sweep of footsteps outside her door. The candle upon her bedside table was out, and the fire that had so merrily crackled within its grate was cold, the coals gray.

Theodora stood and felt her way through the dark, toes curling at the chill of the floorboards. She called out, wondering whether Ottoline perhaps needed her. No answer came and, for a moment, there was silence.

She made her way to the door to peer into the dark, voice echoing as she called out again. While standing upon the threshold of her shadowed bedroom, Theodora caught a glimpse of what appeared to be white skirts disappearing around the corner. "Ottoline!" Her voice rose, weary from being awoken. "I am not one to tolerate pranks."

Out into the darkness she wandered, hand against the heavy wallpaper, feet sweeping along the cold wood floor. In the murky moonlight threading through the thin windows, she spotted the flash of white.

With one hand catching the hem of her nightgown, Theodora quickened her pace. "I will be telling your father, Ottoline! To be out of bed at this hour is unacceptable; you will be in a foul temper tomorrow and, let me tell you this, you'll receive no sympathy from me."

Theodora followed the corridor out onto the main landing, where the staircases swept around and down. There was nothing there. No white skirts or footsteps. Only the empty foyer, grand and quiet and stern.

Moonlight tumbled in from the large window before her and, as she turned, Theodora could plainly see a trail of wet and muddy footprints.

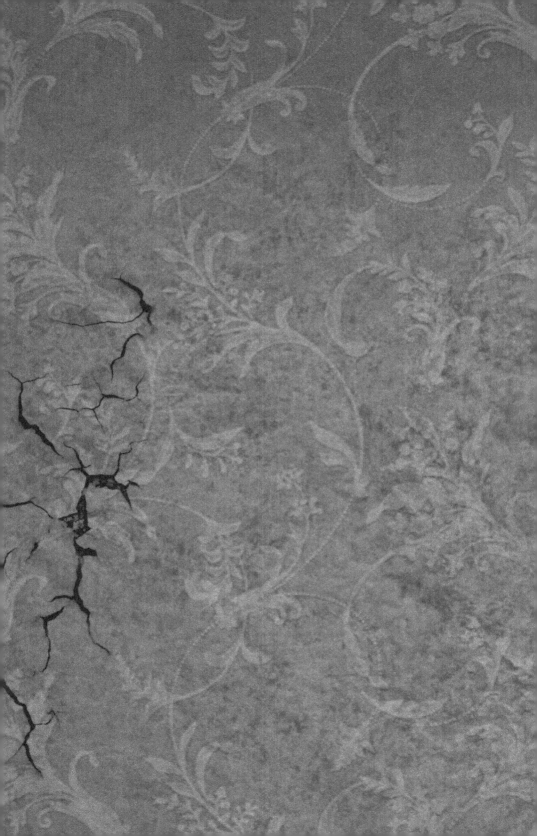

Six

Truth is so rare, it is a delight to tell it

T ea awaited Theodora in the kitchen the following morning.
The room flickered with gentle candlelight and the fire was lit.
Ms. Rivers sat beside it, a crochet hook in one hand and a ball of deep
green yarn in her lap.

"Ottoline was out of bed in the night," Theodora said, taking a
seat beside the stern-faced woman.

Ms. Rivers looked up from her work. "Are you certain it was
her?"

Steam rose from her teacup, a slice of lemon bobbing in it, filling
the room with the scents of citrus and bergamot. "If not Ottoline,
then who? Are there many other servants here, aside from you
and I?"

"It is a big house to keep, Miss Corvus, but I keep it alone and I
do what I can."

"Has Ottoline gone looking for her governesses before? Perhaps
after a bad dream? If she was seeking comfort in the night, I would
like her to know she can come to me. No matter the hour." She

paused. "But if she was playing pranks, I will not tolerate such silliness."

Ms. Rivers continued her crochet, fingers sliding over the colored wool, hook darting in and out and beneath with an expert's grace. "Your previous children," Ms. Rivers began, eyes fixed upon her stitches, "were they ones for pranks?"

"The boy was." Theodora answered truthfully, quietly dreading what sort of man Henry would become. "There was a spiteful streak to him."

"Like his father I have no doubts." Ms. Rivers glanced up, looking at Theodora as though she could see all the secrets she hid. "Servants talk, girl; once upon a time, this house had plenty. It is well known why the Kingswards cannot keep their help."

Theodora sat straighter. "I don't know what you mean."

Ms. Rivers carried on her crochet, eyes down. "Don't you indeed?"

The following silence was filled with the crackle of flames and the soft shuffle of colored wool through the housekeeper's fingers. Theodora kept her hands in her lap, away from the heaviness of her chest, drawing no attention to the weight of feelings she held there. They were for no one else—that grief and loss and longing—and if they were to weigh her down as they grew heavier still, then so be it.

"I would like to meet Lord Thorne today, if his lordship is feeling better," Theodora said into the quiet.

Ms. Rivers set down her crochet to take a long sip of her cooling tea. "I will pass on your request, Miss Corvus."

The lesson with Ottoline took place in her playroom. The winter sun filtered through the tall windows, catching the colored mobiles hung from the curtain rails so they painted rainbows across the dark wood floors.

A large dollhouse stood in one corner, painted a sweet duck-egg blue. Beside it was a rocking horse, beautifully carved from deep black wood. The mane and tail were silver, and its leather reins and saddle were waxed to the highest of shines.

More toys sat upon wooden chests and high upon shelves, dolls and music boxes and books. So many books. It was brighter than the rest of the house, walls a pale blue and the harsh floor covered with rugs edged in gold thread. It was a room that not only spoke to Theodora, it sang.

Ottoline painted at her desk, brush held with great concentration in delicate fingers to replicate the bowl of fruit before her.

"I prefer to paint portraits, Miss Corvus," she said, gently adding a shade of deep red to the green of her apple. "I would have loved to paint yours."

Theodora grimaced at the bruise coloring of the apple on Ottoline's canvas, seeing no such spotting upon the vibrant fruit in the bowl. "We will be studying still-life for a few weeks yet but, when the time comes and if you still want to paint my picture, I will be happy to sit for you."

The girl sulked, a pout on her rosebud lips.

"If you do not like the fruit bowl," Theodora continued, watching the too-wet paint bleed together and drip down the white of the canvas, "you may go outside and collect whatever plant life you can find and paint that."

Ottoline turned to look out the window, at the heavy clouds that had gathered. "It is going to rain."

"Do you not like to get wet, Ottoline?"

"Do you, Miss Corvus?"

The girl did not turn from the window, the tip of her paintbrush dripping bruises over the mottled flesh of her watercolor apple.

"I do not mind—" Theodora began but was interrupted by a tap at the playroom door.

"His lordship is free to see you," Ms. Rivers announced, eyes narrowing at Ottoline's artwork. "A vast improvement, little miss."

If what she achieved that morning was an improvement, Theodora had to wonder how poor the girl's work was before.

~

Once again, Theodora waited in the dimly lit sitting room with the tick of the clock as her only company. She observed the pretty paintings hung from the picture rail: small renditions of herbs, dried flowers, and wild birds. Upon the side tables were delicate carved boxes with golden legs set beside empty silver frames. The room was feminine, gentle and soft but, although it appeared cozy, Theodora could not shake the feeling of abandonment it exuded.

When a knock at the door disturbed the quiet, she expected the stern face of Ms. Rivers to appear. Yet it was not the housekeeper, nor was it Ottoline.

"Miss Corvus? You wished to speak with me?"

Theodora sprang from the comfort of the old armchair, bobbing a curtsy with as much grace as she could muster. She had assumed she was to be called up to the Lord's study, or a library, or some other formal room—not remain in the cramped sitting room with its mismatched chairs and long-forgotten cup of tea.

"Only to introduce myself formally, sir." Theodora collected her wits, back straight, voice steady—just as Grandmother had taught. "And to go over the plans for Ottoline's schooling."

Cassias Thorne took another step into the sitting room, dark eyes flickering in the candlelight. He appeared younger than Theodora had imagined, perhaps only a few years older than herself. He stood tall and rigid; hands curled at his sides as though bracing himself like a loose-rooted tree in a storm. His hair was as dark as his eyes, curling just shy of his shoulder. The suit he wore was fine and expensive, the cravat at his neck pinned tightly with what Theodora guessed was a real ruby.

"You were a governess before?" he asked, voice quiet and soft in the darkness. He did not look at her but turned his gaze to the little fire dancing in the grate.

"I was, sir."

"Then I trust you have knowledge on what children should learn."

"Of course...but there must be areas you would like me to focus on with Ottoline? Where did her last Governess leave her lessons?"

Cassias Thorne at last looked up. "She did not have one."

"Then who—"

"My wife oversaw her education, Miss Corvus, and she has since departed to the coast for her health."

"I really do need a starting point, my lord."

"Have you asked Ottoline?" Cassias Thorne stepped back, retreating from Theodora, gaze once again finding the candlelight. "Of all the people left in this house, I believe she is the one best to ask."

The strange request hung heavy in the air for a beat too long before Theodora answered, "If that is what you wish, my lord. I am happy to oblige."

"There is little joy within these walls, Miss Corvus, for little girls. It is a lonely house, made ever lonelier by the departure of my wife. You were sought for companionship for my daughter, and that is what I ask of you."

Theodora bobbed another curtsy, one that would have made Grandmother proud. "Yes, my lord."

He waved a dismissive hand. "Don't call me that."

"Then what should—"

"Cassias will do."

"I could never!" Theodora said, startled.

"You asked, and I answered," Cassias said, words quick and quiet. "Ms. Rivers refuses because she is too old for change. Since you are new here, I ask you to call me by my given name...I seldom hear it anymore."

"As you wish, my—" Theodora halted and, with a quick nod she continued with a slightly awkward, "Cassias."

The word felt odd against her tongue, both strange and familiar at once. But the young lord inclined his head to her, a wave of soft gratitude easing the harsh lines of his face.

"If that is all, Miss Corvus?"

"If you would allow it...Cassias, and if I am to be on first name terms with yourself, then I insist you call me Theodora."

"A fair request," Cassias answered before backing further away. He reached for the doorknob and, with another quick nod, he left.

It did not go unnoticed that he had not tried out her name, leaving Theodora to wonder whether it would fall clumsy from his lips as his had from hers.

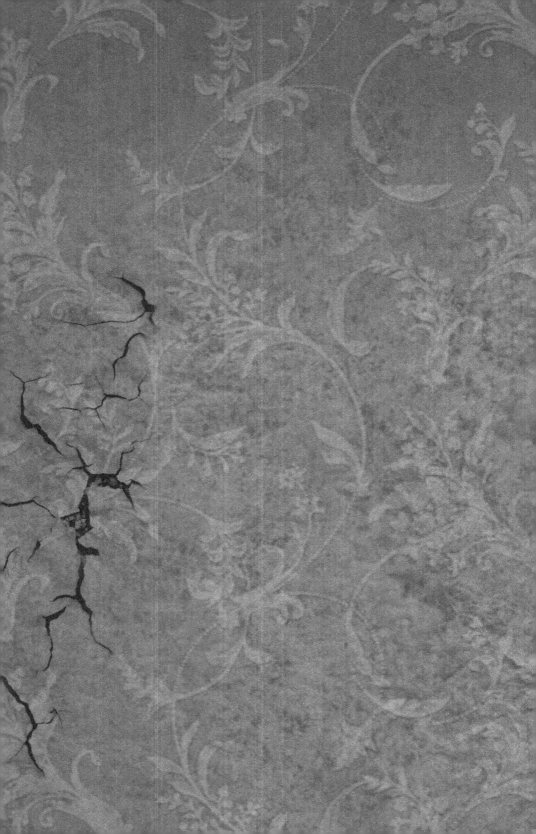

Seven

That in itself is a tremendous thing

The afternoon slipped by, nearly going unnoticed. The gray
skies darkened with more rain, which slowly turned to sleet as
the evening drew in. It soaked into the stone of Broken Oak, marring
the perfect white until the house was as bleak as the winter-stripped
grounds surrounding it.

The candles on the side tables were lit and the fires burned
bright, banishing the shadows of the great house to its far corners as
Theodora settled Ottoline down for bed.

Ottoline's bedroom overlooked the back of the grounds—flat
fields and thin-limbed trees. It was a modest space, not as grand as
many of the other rooms, but perfect in its own right. The bed was
made of carved and polished wood, the sweeping headrest reaching
near the ceiling. Vines and leaves were beautifully etched into
bedposts, the tops pointed so it looked like a miniature fairy castle.

The furnishings around the bed were just as elaborate, all
sweeping wood, carved with gilded leaves and ivy. The handles upon
the armoire, Theodora noticed, were wooden dormice, curled tight

and sleeping, tails locking together to form the latch. An old rocking chair sat beside the bed, furnished with embroidered cushions in rich greens and reds and golds. Along one wall, nestled upon built in shelves painted a deep yellow, sat a row of porcelain dolls. Each wore dresses of silk in pinks and greens and blues, all with matching white shoes and dainty socks. They watched with unblinking painted eyes as Theodora tucked the girl into bed, their faces cold, passive, and unmoving.

She had brushed the tangles from the girl's hair, plumped the fine silk pillows, before returning the firm embrace Ottoline gifted her.

"You are most skilled at hugging, Ottoline," Theodora said, not wishing to be the first to let go. "I dare say this is the best hug I have ever received."

"You are saying that to tease me, Miss Corvus." Ottoline's muffed words hummed against her shoulder before she pulled back, a lovely smile at her lips.

"Perhaps." Theodora tapped her on the nose, earning a broader smile, then said, in all seriousness. "You didn't happen to go running down the halls last night, did you, Ottoline?"

The girl climbed beneath the covers, pulling the heavy quilts up to her chin. "It is dark at night, Miss Corvus. I don't like to go out in the dark."

"And you wouldn't lie to me?"

Ottoline shook her head, eyes darting to the bedroom door before landing once again on her governess. "I don't like the dark, and I don't like the cold, Miss Corvus."

"I believe you, Ottoline." Theodora tucked the edges of her blankets in tight. "We will say no more about it."

"I wish you could stay here, Miss Corvus."

"The fire is bright tonight, Ottoline, and I am not so very far away." Theodora brushed the golden curls away from the girl's face, pausing for a moment more to tuck the covers tighter around her small frame. "Goodnight, Ottoline."

"Goodnight, Miss Corvus." She wound her fingers around Theodora's hand and squeezed. "I am so very glad you are here."

Theodora brought the small hand to her lips before tucking it beneath the warmth of the covers. "As am I, Ottoline."

~

Theodora left Ms. Rivers bent double over her crochet in the kitchen, eyes narrowed as she worked in the dim light.

Theodora wandered along the candlelit corridors, exploring parts of the house she had not seen in the daylight. She found herself in a gallery of sorts—the room was wide and long with velvet chairs lining the walls, deep crimson with gold tassels that hung in glittering knots from the seat pads. More paintings in gilded frames rested along the walls, portraits of grim-faced men and stern women stared down at her, lips pinched, faces wan. She recognized the gentleman in one she passed, a younger likeness. Dark eyes stared from a pale face though, unlike the others, they did not stare down at her but focused, it seemed, over her shoulder.

With a sense of unease, Theodora followed its gaze to the painted face of a woman. Soft waves of chestnut hair fell over her shoulders and white gown. The painted green of her eyes was fixed upon Theodora, the lift of her lips suggesting she was surveying the governess and had found her lacking.

"My beloved wife."

Theodora startled, hand flying quicker than her thoughts. Her palm struck the cheek of her employer with a damning thwack.

His eyes widened, fingers touching the edge of his face. His mouth gaped. "You hit me!"

"You frightened me!" An apology lingered at the tip of her tongue, but she swallowed it. "It is rude to sneak up on people."

"I was not sneaking up on you, Theodora," he replied, hand still at his cheek. "You were loitering...in the shadows."

She knew she was doing no such thing. "I was looking at the portraits."

"Did you not have portraits at your home?"

"Pardon? Of course, we had portraits at Woodrow House." Theodora did not add that many of them had crumbled to nothing due to the damp, and the ones that had survived were mold-covered, the frames riddled with woodworm. "I have not seen these portraits before; they are exquisite."

Cassias Thorne followed Theodora's gaze, reaching for the delicate brush strokes of his wife's gown. He paused just before he touched the canvas, fingers hovering a breath away from the brushstrokes. "This was painted not long before she fell ill and took to the seaside; she did dearly love that dress."

"I hope she returns soon and in good health, Cassias. I am sure you and Ottoline must miss her terribly."

"Sometimes I wonder if she will return at all," Cassias replied, eyes fixed upon Lady Thorne's unforgiving stare. "Her illness came on so suddenly, you see. Perhaps brought on by the dampness in these old walls, or from the chill of the bedroom window that just won't seem to close right. I feel it too, sometimes; a closeness to the air, a coldness that settles in the bones. We had tea one evening, and I remember it being all rather lovely. We seldom made time for it, but there we were with little cakes and a full teapot." He took a breath and sighed. "But to the coast Eleanor went, and we remain."

"Would she send for Ottoline, then?" Theodora asked, thinking of the way the girl had clung to her that evening—the hug so sorely needed. "To have her daughter join her at the seaside? To have you both for company? I know for certain she would love such a trip."

"Rose, Ottoline's mother, died when she was six," Cassias said, turning to Theodora. "I remarried the following year. I was hoping to...to fill a void carved out by her absence. I was ill prepared for the void that Ottoline could not fill for Eleanor." His hand went to his mouth, knuckles at his lips. "Forgive me...it has been too long without company, Miss Corvus. I beg you not to think ill of my wife or of me, for that matter, for my over-familiarity."

Theodora reached across the small span of darkness between them, hand for a most fleeting of moments brushing against his sleeve. "I am an orphan, Lord Thorne; I understand grief, and I understand the longing for someone who is not and will not ever be present again." She paused, smiling slightly. "You asked me here to be a friend to Ottoline and that I will do with every beat of my heart. And, if I could be bold, as you were, I could also be a friend to you. This is a large and lonely house; let it just be large."

Cassias stared up at the portrait of his wife, meeting her eyes as though daring her to look away first. It was an odd look, one that Theodora could not quite place, unsure if it was one of longing, one of grief or sorrow or something else entirely.

"I would not object to friendship, Theodora," Cassias said at last. "Though I must warn you that I am neither a person of interest nor one for casual conversation. I fear you will find me a boring friend."

"There are worse things to be, Cassias."

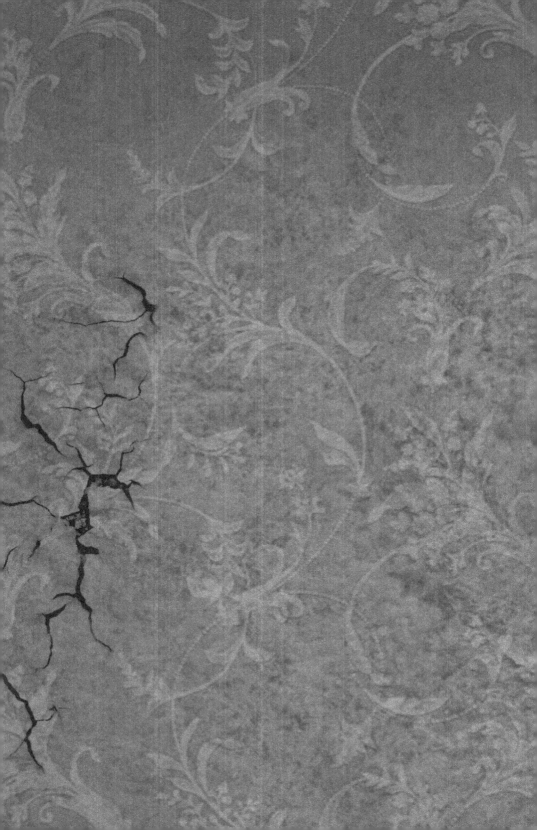

Eight

But he who does not grasp the thorn

S leep withheld its claim on Theodora; she lay upon the soft
sheets, beneath the fine blankets, and stared out into the
growing dark. The fire in her grate burned low, the candles long
extinguished. The house stood quiet, surrounding Theodora with its
silence, its darkness, and its well-kept secrets. She found herself
longing for the crumbling walls of Woodrow House. She missed the
pipes that echoed its rumblings every time it rained, missed the
shifting of its foundations, the crumble of brittle stone. She missed
the way it kept not a single secret from her, but laid them bare within
its skeletal timbers: a shared truth that time and age came for all.

From her bed, she listened, straining to hear the slightest of whispers—and there it was, nearly nothing...a hint of a creaking floor-
board. Theodora slipped from her bed, feet soundless upon the
wood, and peered out into the heavy black corridor. Another creak, a
soft moan, the sound of skirts sighing around quick feet.

"Ottoline!" Theodora called, but the flash of white skirts did not
slow. With her own gathered in her hand, she followed down the

dark hallways, other hand braced along the wall. "Ottoline, I know it is you."

She found herself in the gallery where she had bumped into Cassias, the portraits illuminated by the white glow of the moonlight. It cast shadows where there had been none before, resting against the sharp edges of Eleanor Thorne. Bathed in moonglow, her gown was ethereal in its softness; the white so pure that she could not make out a single brushstroke. The softness ended at the lace neckline, as though the artist wished to show the juxtaposition between the delicate garment and the cold cut of the woman wearing it.

Taking a step back from Lady Thorne's unyielding gaze, Theodora slipped, and braced herself against the gilt frame. She turned, the moonlight catching the wet footprints that had followed her through the dark and come to rest before Eleanor's portrait.

"Ottoline?" Theodora called into the dark. "If it is you out of bed, come now and we will go back together, and not a word will I speak of it to your father."

In the shadows, beneath the moonlight, there came no answer—no soft whisper, no creaks or groans—just the silence of an old house that held its secrets close.

With another cautious glance at the muddied footprints, Theodora turned away from Lady Thorne and hurried back to bed. She settled herself under the thin, scratchy blankets and closed her eyes. The fire burned low, the flames flickering gently, its glow one of softness and calm. Theodora thought herself foolish, startled by the shadows that all old houses created. She huffed and turned over, her back to the door. And there, within that comfortable dark she heard it, the turn of the latch, the slow creaking of the door as it swayed open. The sound of footsteps followed, the scrape of boots across the floor. She lay unmoving, breath held, turning only when she felt the brush of a hand against the covers. Darkness welcomed her, an empty space made greater still by the open doorway. Darkness and nothing more.

The morning drew in without rain and, much to Ottoline's delight, Theodora took her lessons outside. With the girl's hand tight in hers, they walked around the lilypond to the rose garden on the other side of the grounds. There were no blooms—not even buds upon the thorny stems—but, though the garden slept, it held a promise of what could be, given time. Leaves and debris littered the narrow, winding paths, the dried husks of old seed pods blowing along the stone in the wind. Weeds had long choked the more delicate flowers, taking over anything unfit for winter. Theodora admired that about plants, weeds or otherwise; the tenacity of ugly things.

"The gardener left a while back," Ottoline said, small hand brushing the dew-soaked threads of an abandoned cobweb. "She never liked roses."

"Who didn't?"

"My stepmother." The strands of silk broke beneath Ottoline's finger, its weaver long gone or long dead. "She thought them common."

"And what do you think of them, Ottoline?"

The girl plucked a dried bud from a frost-weakened stem and tossed it into a hedge. "I like the way they guard their prettiness with sharp edges."

Theodora regarded the girl for a moment in comfortable silence, wondering if perhaps she would grow to be beautiful and sharp—if she would need to be when the time came to take a husband and keep a house of her own.

"What are your favorite flowers, Miss Corvus?"

"I like daisies, Ottoline. Fields and fields of white flowers on a hot summer's day."

Ottoline laughed, one gloved hand coming up to hide her grin. "Now *they* are common. And widely thought of as weeds."

"I love the abundance of them, the way they will flourish anywhere with no help from human hands," Theodora replied, smiling. "They grow where they please, taking no heed of the strict, rigid lawns of grand houses."

"You could say that about any weed, Miss Corvus."

"You could indeed, Ottoline." Theodora gave her ward a gentle nudge. "I have an affinity for things that refuse to know their place."

The smile slipped from the girl's face, her hand rising to close around Theodora's. "My place is here, Miss Corvus. I know that as sure as anything."

"For now, perhaps, but who knows where the wind will blow you?"

Ottoline looked down at her boots, toes scraping over the stone. "My roots are quite deep in Broken Oak soil. I think I am happy with that."

Theodora could not argue, for she knew how grounded one could be in their home, the familiarity of it. Her father had wished so much more for her, the way she wished more for Ottoline, but Theodora had instead grown up in the house he had abandoned and had only fled to avoid scandal.

Where would she have gone, had her father remained? What would she have become with his gentle voice guiding her to be more, something other than a governess, a guardian of children more fortunate than she? Theodora often wondered if her father would have been disappointed by the life she chose—for choosing to remain at Woodrow with its sinking foundations, black-eyed ghosts, and the old woman who would not die. But as much as her father despised the old house, it was a part of Theodora, and she could not shake the longing for it. Would he then be disappointed that she had left Woodrow House, only to find another large mansion to hide in?

But her father was long dead and gone, naught but bone beneath the cold earth, and could hold no such thoughts about her. He was gone and had not waited for her, and the weight of that now fit quite comfortably at her breast. It did no good to anyone to dwell upon the thoughts and hopes of those departed.

"I see you are admiring my rose garden." Cassias Thorne's black boots made no sound upon the stone paving. He stopped beside a creeping rose, threading the thin stalks around the trellis it was trying to escape from. "These should have been cut back, and I fear it is too late for them now. Are you fond of roses, Theodora?"

"She prefers daisies," Ottoline answered with a grin.

"Does she indeed?" Cassias returned her smile, face softening as she stepped away from Theodora and into his arms. "Then you will love the lawn in summer; they bloom here in abundance."

Theodora took in the easy affection of father and child, the way Ottoline fit against his body as though truly a piece of him. His hand rested against the small of her back, easy and natural. It tugged at the stone in her chest, poked at the grief hidden so very carefully there. She swallowed that feeling and kept it close and smiled in return.

"A summer filled with daisy chain crowns awaits us then," she said, tucking another stalk behind the trellis, weaving it behind the one Cassias had threaded through. "You could make a special one for your stepmother, Ottoline, when she is well again."

"There is nothing quite so healing as the air down at the coast," Cassias said, dropping his arm from Ottoline. "I am sure my wife will be home soon."

"Will I stay on after?" Theodora asked, before realizing the rudeness of her question. "I mean, if I am to be let go once your wife returns, I would need some notice so I can look for other placements."

"You won't leave here, Miss Corvus," Ottoline said, small fingers plucking more dead seed-heads from the flower beds. "Will she, Father?"

"It...it will be likely that you will be needed for some time, if it suits you?"

Theodora smiled down at Ottoline. "It suits me just fine."

"Then you will stay?" Ottoline said, clasping Theodora's hands. Her eyes were wide, hopeful and bright. "For always, Miss Corvus?"

"I cannot stay for always, Ottoline." Theodora laughed. "But I will remain as long as I am able."

"Where will you go, then?" the girl asked. "When you leave me behind?"

"Ottoline—" Cassias admonished, the gentle tone of his voice failing to catch his daughter's notice.

"I will go home," Theodora began, "One day, I will go home, Ottoline."

The girl folded her arms across her chest, her chin lifted, mouth petulant. "No, you won't."

"Do not speak to Miss Corvus so, Ottoline." The gentleness slipped from Cassias' voice, though still there was no hardness to it, no anger. "Apologize at once."

"I shan't!" Ottoline's bottom lip wobbled. She turned and stomped away, feet as soundless as her father's had been. They watched her go, disappearing from the rose garden toward the stone steps of Broken Oak.

"Perhaps," Cassias said, with a cautious glance toward the house, "Perhaps I should not have raised my voice."

Theodora schooled her face, only just stopping herself from scoffing aloud. "If we are to be friends, Cassias, please allow me to be bold."

The young lord nodded. "Am I too hard on her?"

"I fear you coddle her," Theodora said quickly, moving on before he could continue. "I doubt you have ever raised your voice to that child in her life, am I correct?"

"I...I have."

"With the greatest of respect, Cassias, I sincerely doubt you."

His smile was sheepish. "Eleanor would always be firmer, but I cannot find it within me to scold a girl who has lost a mother."

"Boundaries still need to be in place, Cassias, else that darling child of yours will become quite the handful."

"A part of me wants to see that wildness grow." His eyes darted to hers as though he were sharing a daring secret. "To see if it takes her to places no woman has stepped before."

Theodora shared his smile, looking toward where Ottoline had disappeared into the house. It was rare to listen to a father reluctant to clip his daughter's wings. "You would allow that for her? Truly?"

"The world needs less well-mannered women, Theodora."

She held a hand to her breast. "What a scandalous thing to say."

"Have I offended you, then?"

"Perhaps," Theodora replied, her smile unfaltering. "Am I one of these ill-mannered women you speak of? Or am I another woman who will leave not a mark upon this earth?"

He turned to her, all dark eyes and a soft smile. "Miss Corvus, as a gentleman, you must know I cannot answer that."

"As a gentleman, no, but as a friend you must. I insist."

"I would like to get better acquainted with you before I make judgment on your manners," Cassias said. "Some evenings, Ms. Rivers and I sit in the sitting room, and it's good company. I know it ought not be done, but no one comes to this god-awful house anymore and it is horribly lonely...and, if you would like to join us before retiring to your room for the night, I would enjoy your company."

Theodora looked toward the shadows of Broken Oak Manor, to the dark windows, to the cold perfection of the stone, and thought about how easily a house so large could swallow a person whole.

"I would like that, Cassias," she replied, "Thank you."

"Try not to allow the shadows of this house to unnerve you," he said, turning to perch on the low stone wall surrounding the roses. "Or the strangeness of our manners here."

Theodora joined him on the wall, careful not to catch her hair or dress upon the thorns at her back. "I think I will come to prefer the companionship of this house, Cassias. It is...refreshing after how it was at Kingsward Manor."

"I am guessing the Lord Kingsward acted as a lord should act?"

She drew her arms around herself, holding tight. "You could say he did."

"I was never much good at it." He twisted a stem around in his fingers, the stalk blackened and dead. "Eleanor would chide me for being too soft on the staff, but I enjoyed their happiness, the songs they sang while they worked, the smiles they shared as they passed by."

"Why did they leave?"

He shrugged. "Their reasoning is lost on me. It seems as though one day the house grew suddenly quiet and empty without me realizing."

Theodora stood, brushing off her skirts, waiting for Cassias to rise beside her. "I am always keen to work with a smile, though I confess you will not catch me singing."

"A sad declaration indeed, Miss Corvus." Laughter brightened his words, real and honest. It left Theodora with a warmth around her heart, a feeling that she would truly learn to belong. That Broken Oak, with time and acceptance, could be just as much home to her as Woodrow.

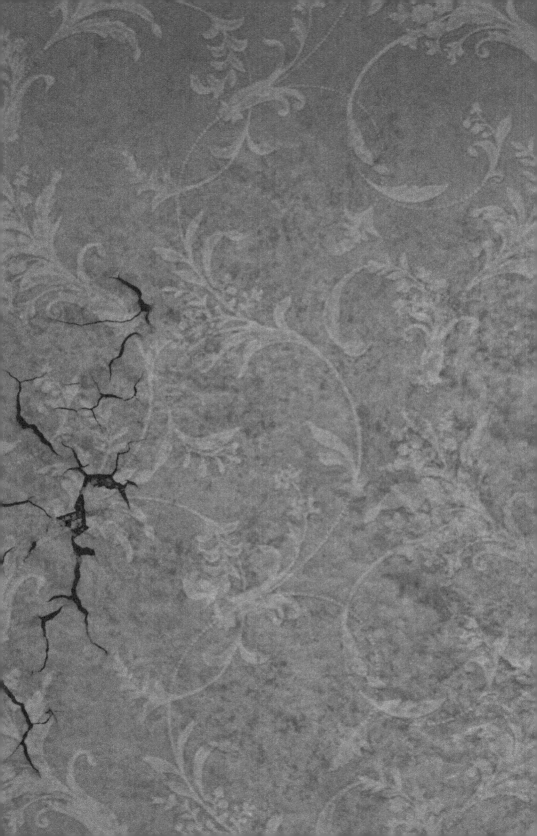

Nine

Half savage and hardy and free

There were no watchers by the pond at Broken Oak, no black-eyed specters with their silent smiles. They had not followed her to Broken Oak and Theodora felt their absence. No matter that the faces of her father and mother were not among them, it was the lack of looking that haunted her. The emptiness.

There were no watchers, but Theodora felt watched all the same. The neat rows of painted faces bore down on her from Ottoline's shelf, their dresses starched and stiff.

"That is Angelica," Ottoline said, pointing to the first doll. "Then Harriet, Jane, and Elizabeth. I put Juliet away in the toybox over there for being naughty."

"Oh? And what did naughty Juliet do?" Theodora asked, noting there was no room on the shelf to fit another doll. "May I at least meet poor Juliet? Your other dolls are so fine, I am curious to see what a mischievous doll looks like."

She moved over to the toybox, reaching in for the exiled doll. It looked much the same as the others, pale-faced and beautifully dressed. The blonde corkscrew curls were glossy, the glass eyes shining, little shoes polished and perfect.

"She keeps me awake some nights with the tapping, so I had to move her."

"What tapping?"

Ottoline reached out a hand and pushed the arm of the rocking chair beside her bed. It creaked forward, then back, the headrest hitting the wall behind with a dull tap. "I cannot sleep when she is tapping, Miss Corvus."

Back into the darkness the doll went before Theodora placed a hand upon the chair, halting its rocking. "You have a wonderful imagination, Ottoline! Perhaps you should be a writer when you grow up?"

The girl smiled. "Do you think so?"

Theodora pulled the blankets up tight, plumping the pillows behind Ottoline's head. "You can be whatever you dream of being."

"Did you dream of being a governess, Miss Corvus?" Ottoline asked, turning her back to the wall of dolls and the rocking chair.

"In all honesty, I did not. It found me, Ottoline, as dreams sometimes do."

"Are you happy here? With us?"

"I am."

"You won't leave."

"Not for a while, Ottoline."

"You won't," the girl replied.

"Ottoline," Theodora said, one hand resting against the rocking chair. "Were you out of bed last night? Near my room?"

"I don't like going out in the dark, Miss Corvus."

Theodora held the girl's stare, waiting for her to continue. Ottoline said nothing. "Are you sure? I won't be cross if you tell me the truth now."

"Perhaps it was a ghost, Miss Corvus, I hear this house is full of them."

"Very amusing, Ottoline. Do not let me catch you out of bed

again, do you understand me?" Theodora was used to childish games, but had little patience for them in the dead of night.

"I won't be out of bed, I promise."

Theodora swept a curl from Ottoline's forehead, tucking it behind her ear with care. The girl closed her eyes, dark eyelashes stark against the paleness of her skin. "I am glad to hear it. Goodnight, Ottoline."

"Goodnight, Miss Corvus."

The sitting room was awash in gentle candlelight—the fireplace full and hearty. It was one of the more formal lounging rooms, filled with fat sofas and well-crafted bookshelves. Rugs adorned the polished floors, soft underfoot. It was not as cozy as her little sanctuary, but it held a surprising warmth to it—a goodness that had seeped into the wallpaper.

Theodora sat beside Ms. Rivers, who had abandoned her crochet and instead held a dainty teacup in her clever fingers. Cassias reclined in one of the many armchairs, head tilted back, legs outstretched.

"This truly is a magnificent house, Cassias," Theodora said, one hand running over the green velvet cushions.

"It is far too big," he replied from his relaxed position by the fire. "My great-great grandfather had it built to impress Lady Nightingale in the hope of marrying her. He built a new wing every time she declined him."

"This house is enormous." Theodora let out a laugh. "How many times did she reject him before agreeing?"

"My dear Theodora, she never accepted his desperate attempts at wooing her. The great Lord Thorne was forced to marry a woman of far inferior birth before his old heart gave out, and he was left without an heir."

Ms. Rivers spooned sugar into her tea, looking over the rim toward the young lord. "It was your grandfather, I believe, who had most of the north wing built—not to woo his intended but to escape his overbearing wife."

Theodora raised her brows at the impertinence of the housekeeper, but Cassias laughed as though no ill will was taken. "My grandmother was a terrifying woman, indeed. I cannot blame the man for hiding from her." He sat up, meeting Theodora's startled gaze. "Ah, Ms. Rivers, I do believe we may have horrified dear Theodora with our slander of my ancestors."

The housekeeper put her teacup down, narrow eyes fixed upon Theodora. "I have quite the many scandalous stories of the former occupants of this house, Miss Corvus, if your delicate ears would not object to hearing them."

She was being teased—she was well aware of that and found that she did not mind. There was a gentle fondness to it, the words laced with good humor and not malice.

"Your stories intrigue me, Ms. Rivers, and I am far from horrified. My surprise is only from the way you are with each other, servant and lord. I know we spoke of it a little, Cassias, in the rose garden but it is very unusual, almost like you are..." She trailed off, unsure of the comparison.

"Like family?" Cassias finished for her. "Perhaps it is strange and unheard of in most other grand houses. I do not doubt that I would be the topic of gossip at many a dinner party but, since I do not go to any, I find I care not a bit about what others may think."

"Was your wife of a similar mind?"

Cassias kept her gaze, the firelight dancing in his dark eyes. "Which one?"

Theodora thought of the painting of the stern-faced woman, the rigidness of her mouth, the sharpness of her eyes. "The present Lady Thorne."

The smile dimmed, only slightly, the barest tightening of his lips. "Eleanor had a more traditional outlook on life, where people knew their place and kept it."

"And the former?"

It was Ms. Rivers who answered, hands in her lap, eyes closed. Almost wistful. "Rose would dine with the maids, dance with the footmen and gossip like an old fishwife with the gardeners."

"Do you remember old Cook?" Cassias interjected. "How she used to scold her for getting beneath her feet when the supper was on. Whacked her more than once for getting underfoot." The smile bloomed at Cassias's mouth, his body leaning forward to share his memories with Ms. Rivers.

"The cook hit your wife?" Theodora exclaimed, a half-laugh upon her tongue. "Hit the lady of the house and kept her position here?"

Ms. Rivers pointed at Theodora. "There is someone who has never tasted Cook's apple tarts. You don't dismiss talent like that."

"I do miss those tarts," Cassias sighed. "Theodora, they were made with the ripest of apples, stewed with hot cider before baking beneath a crust so golden I am sure you could gilt the woodwork with it. They were spiced with cinnamon and nutmeg, a hint of ginger if I am not mistaken, and sprinkled with enough brown sugar to make one's teeth rot."

"The scent of them was divine," Ms. Rivers agreed. "It was a happier time."

Theodora nodded, truly believing the words. "I still find it astonishing that the cook would hit the lady of the house."

"My darling Rose did not possess the hardness of heart to dismiss, discipline, or rule any servants this house kept," Cassias said, voice soft. "It shocked many, and she did not care. Many times, I was asked to bring my wife to heel, as though she were a disobedient dog. The house was clean, the food hot, the servants and my wife happy, so why would I wish to change that? It was a good home, Miss Corvus. For a few fleeting years, this was a good home."

The use of her title did not go unnoticed by Theodora. She wondered if, perhaps, he felt her name, and that of his wife, were best kept distanced from each other. The laughter was gone, the merriment seeping back into the walls like water into a sponge. The house seemed to draw it in, locking secrets and memories away as Theodora did her own.

"I would have loved to have met her," Theodora said, leaning forward. She was not close enough to reach across to Cassias and would not have been bold enough to do so even if she were. But she hoped that the little closeness she could offer would do something to dampen the sorrow that had replaced his easy smile.

"I have no doubt you would have been good friends, Theodora," he replied, leaning forward himself. "Tell me more of the house you worked in before."

She stilled, straightening her back. "There is not much more to tell."

"Kingsward is far down south, is it not, Miss Corvus? Not too far from your family home." Ms. Rivers asked.

"That is correct. Woodrow House and Kingsward Manor are separated by only a few miles. I worked at Kingsward for nearly three years before I was no longer needed, and we parted ways."

Ms. Rivers nodded. "So far from home."

Theodora pressed her hands into her lap, swallowing the longing for a place no longer hers. "Yes, so far from home."

"May I ask why?" Cassias asked, arms resting upon his knees, fingers steepled to rest his chin upon.

"Why I became a governess?"

"You can answer that too, if you wish," Cassias said, "but why take up a position so very far away?"

Theodora paused, unhappy with the course of the conversation. "Is there a geographical restriction on where one can seek employment?"

"Of course not," Cassias answered. "I am only curious. Do you leave behind any family?"

"My grandmother, Cassias." Theodora could not quite help the frostiness of her tone. "My only living family, and it was she who encouraged this setting. This adventure."

"So far away from her?"

"I believe we have well established I have journeyed far away from my home, Cassias. Goodness me! You sought a governess, and here I am!"

"I quite forgot we had answered an advertisement, it seems your grandmother was seeking an alternative position for you while you were still at Kingsward." He glanced over at Ms. Rivers, who shrugged. "How long have we waited? I had almost given up hope of finding someone for Ottoline and had resolved to send the girl out into the wilds. Truth be told, I sent the letter without my wife knowing, I believed I wanted to be more assertive, more in control. It was a relief when I did not hear back."

"Then you are most fortunate that I am here now."

The truth settled uncomfortably with Theodora, how her grandmother had sought out employment for her elsewhere, for heavens knew how long. How, despite wishing that her granddaughter would become more than a governess, she had come to the conclusion she would be anything but. She had expected a scandal, and had planned accordingly. Begrudgingly, Theodora had to respect the canny old woman's foresight.

"Indeed, we are, Miss Corvus," Miss Rivers said from her armchair, eyes still closed against the gentle warmth of the fireplace.

"I am grateful for you, Theodora, and I do hope you will be happy here." Cassias caught her eye. "I simply wondered if perhaps you were running from something...or someone?"

Theodora stood, shocked, horrified. "I am running from no one, Lord Thorne! Is it so hard to believe that I could wish to see more of the world, nothing more and nothing less? To insult me by suggesting I have some sordid secret—"

Cassias also stood. Ms. Rivers remained seated, eyes open and alert. "I never said you were hiding anything sordid, I said nothing of the sort."

"It was implied." Theodora hissed.

"Then the blame lies with you, Miss Corvus," Cassias snapped, eyes dark, smile gone. "And not me if you have taken my words for something else entirely."

For a moment, nothing else was said—the silence heavy and unkind. Theodora wanted to draw it back and keep it close, to save it from slipping into the walls. That silence, that anger, she did not want the house to have it.

Gathering her skirts, her thoughts, the ache in her throat, Theodora marched from the room, the last few words sharp upon her tongue. "Goodnight, Lord Thorne. Ms. Rivers."

The anger simmered, settling heavily in her stomach like a too-rich meal. Theodora held onto it though, allowing herself to seethe and sulk within the confines of her room. She held onto it to save herself from the thought that perhaps she had taken offence where none was given. If her words were sharp because of the memories he had evoked, then Theodora was happy enough to lay blame upon the young lord; better that than risk stirring the feelings atrophying around her heart.

With her mind not ready to rest, Theodora sat at her desk, to write another letter to her grandmother. She was unsure of what to say, seeking comfort, yet knowing her grandmother was not one to bestow it often. No heartfelt advice would be given either; her grandmother would most likely scold her for speaking out of turn and demand that she apologize. They were not the words Theodora wanted.

She startled and dripped black ink upon the unmarked paper when there came a tapping at her bedroom door.

For a moment, she thought it was Cassias come to her bedchambers to apologize. She remained still, thinking, standing only when the knock came again, harder.

"Who is it?" Theodora demanded.

"Who the devil do you think, Miss Corvus?" Ms. Rivers's shrill voice seeped through the closed door.

With a sigh, Theodora allowed the woman in. "If you have come to scold me about my rudeness, I am in no mood to hear it."

"Oh hush!" The old housekeeper took a seat at Theodora's desk, eyes scanning the ruined paper. "I came to check all was well, Miss Corvus. Despite what you may think, I take no delight in seeing my staff upset."

"I am not upset."

"Indeed." She plucked the pen from the desk and placed it with care back into its holder. "I have an idea as to why you are so far away from your home and your grandmother. I have heard of many members of staff leave Kingsward Manor, moved away quickly and quietly without a fuss. I hear a lot, Miss Corvus, even all the way up here. His Lordship, spoiled and privileged as he is, has no idea— could not begin to fathom the darkness and shadows you hide and keep. You are new and exciting, and he is bored and lonely."

"So, he does not seek friendship then? I am merely an amusement?"

Ms. Rivers pursed her lips, hands in her lap. "You are a governess, Miss Corvus. You are here for Ottoline, do not forget that."

"I have not." Theodora shook her head, standing over the old housekeeper. "You have nothing to fear from me, Ms. Rivers. I shall keep my respectful distance from Lord Thorne."

Ms. Rivers stood, one hand lingering on the stack of writing paper at Theodora's desk. "I ask that you take care, Miss Corvus, that is all."

"Then I appreciate the concern for my well-being."

"I can send the letter when you finish it, Miss Corvus," the housekeeper said as a farewell, nodding at the papers.

The kindness was not lost on Theodora, sharp as it was. "Thank you."

The door clicked quietly behind her, footsteps fading over the wood flooring until Theodora was left alone with more thoughts than she had started out with. With a frustrated sigh, she went back to her desk, pulled out a fresh piece of writing paper and wrote.

Dearest Grandmother,

I do so hope that this letter finds you well. I have not received a reply to my last correspondence and hope to blame the abysmal postal service this far north. I pray that you are in good health, and the house is keeping you well. I miss you both. Yes! I miss Woodrow with every beat of my heart, Father would be appalled! This house, Grandmother, it will not speak to me, I cannot feel it as I did Woodrow and, the harder I try to listen, the quieter it becomes.

I have settled in well, I think. Ottoline is a sweet girl, and I just know you would love her. I have met Lord Thorne, and he seems a caring sort of gentleman, but he is abrupt and I dare say a little odd. I feel the absence of his wife is doing him little favor. I fear he has quite forgotten how to be a proper gentleman and propriety has left with Lady Thorne.

Please do send word when this letter reaches you and know that I send you all my love and best wishes.

Your loving granddaughter,
Theodora

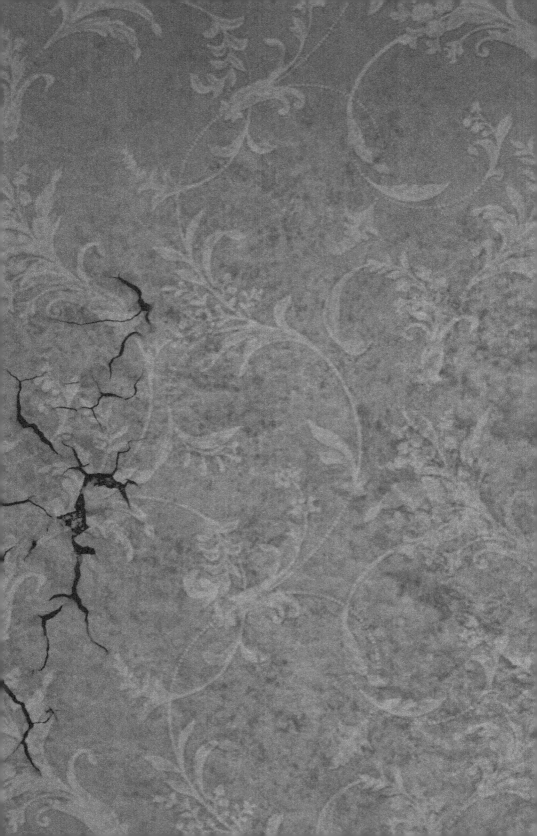

Ten

One for sorrow

Cassias Thorne stood waiting for Theodora the next morning, leaning with casual grace against the kitchen door frame as though he did it often. Ms. Rivers was nowhere to be seen, her teacup absent, her crochet sitting idle upon her chair in the corner. Their eyes met, a bated silence between them weighted down by words unsaid. Theodora dropped into a polite curtsy and sat to wait for Ottoline.

"That's it?" Cassias asked, arms folding against his chest. "One small quarrel and we are no longer friends?"

Theodora chose her words carefully. "I think perhaps it is for the best, Lord Thorne. To seek friendship where it is unlikely to last is foolish at best."

He stood straighter, arms still folded tight against his chest. "Then surely you will never know true friendship, if you squash it down for fear of it not lasting."

"It will not last here," she said. "Ottoline will grow up and have no more need for me; your wife may come home and decide to take charge of Ottoline's tutoring, and I will be sent on my way."

"That is unlikely!"

"That she will come home or send me away?"

He paused, flustered. "She did not say when she would return."

"Have you spoken to her since? Does she not send letters?" Theodora questioned, temper simmering.

"You must be aware that the postal service here is quite appalling," Cassias replied, hands knotting together. "She will return when she is well enough and that will suffice."

"You do not seem to like speaking of your wife, Lord Thorne..."

"I do not like bickering, Theodora, and you seem to enjoy it." Theodora opened her mouth, a retort sharp upon her tongue, but he cut her off, his voice rising. "You are...you are quite the outspoken woman!"

Her laugh burst unbidden and coarse past her lips. "Outspoken woman! Indeed, Lord Thorne, I am, and I have been called worse by my own grandmother. Come now, while we are quarrelling so, tell me some other names you wish to call me."

He was silent a moment, hands slipping into his pockets to stop their fumbling. "You are mocking me."

Theodora regarded the gentleman with the keen sense she had inherited from her grandmother. He stood unsure, not angry or even frustrated, but lost and bemused. Spoiled and lonely, Ms. Rivers had said, and perhaps she was right; but he had asked her for friendship and it felt cruel to deny him such a simple thing as her companionship.

"Humor me, Lord Thorne," she said, leaning forward, hands clasped upon her knees.

He swallowed. "I do not know you well enough to make assumptions, Miss Corvus."

She noted the use of her title and smiled. "But enough to call me outspoken? Enough to imply I have dark little secrets hidden beneath my skirts?"

He glanced at her knees, eyes wide. "I never referred to your skirts!"

When at last his wife returned, he would no longer have need for her friendship; propriety and tradition would no doubt trickle back in and drown out such nonsense. Theodora had to wonder whether she had room left within her overfull heart to take the ache that would no doubt come.

Ms. Rivers was right, of course; Theodora could not argue otherwise. Yet the house was too large, too lonely, too quiet not to clasp the hand of companionship when it was offered.

"Could you truly be friends with an outspoken woman, Cassias? I fear I cannot pretend to be anything but."

They shared a look, a quiet glance, one of waiting and hope.

"I will be glad of the company, Theodora," he said at last, eyes still fixed on hers. "No matter how freely the words fall from your mouth. And, with that, I will respect that the past you carry is your own, and you need not speak of it with me. I only ask if you would also return that sentiment in kind."

The sprawling house kept secrets and she kept secrets, and the lord of the house kept secrets—each folding them into their foundations, curling their bodies around the growing weight. The eaves creaked where the rest of the house stood silent like the bones in Theodora's chest.

Theodora cast her gaze to the window, at the dreary skies and damp fog. Everything beyond the glass slumbered, stark and bare, dressed only in early morning shadows and mist.

"If the drizzle clears up by lunch," Theodora said, not turning from the view of the miserable morning, "I thought Ottoline and I could take our lessons by the pond again today. Perhaps you would like to join us?"

"If the sun shines by midday, Theodora, I would be delighted."

"You have a wonderful daughter, Cassias," Theodora said, enjoying the comfort of the morning light and the gentle sound of rain. "She truly is a credit to you."

"I see her mother in her," Cassias answered, looking out beyond the gray skies. "Not just in looks, but in her mannerisms, the joy she finds in everything around her, how quick she is to love."

"Are those not qualities you hold?"

He looked up, eyes guarded. "To be quick to love?"

"To find joy in the things around you, Cassias? The house? The gardens?"

"Perhaps I once did."

"What changed?" The question slipped from her lips, bold and prying, yet instead of calling it back, she waited to see if the lord of the house would answer.

Cassias kept his gaze on the window, to the low and moody clouds drifting by outside. "My first wife...my Rose..." He stumbled over the words. "I felt as though a lot of life left this house when she passed, Theodora. I tried to fix it, to fill it up again, and I do not believe I have done a very good job."

"We try our best," Theodora said softly. "We can do no more than that. The mistakes we make, the missteps, we learn from them. We only fail when we give up."

He smiled then, a faint pull at the corners of his mouth. "A hopeful sentiment, Theodora, thank you."

She nodded back, turning to leave. "Do not forget to join us later, if the weather brightens."

~

The rain did stop by midmorning. Though the dull and heavy clouds remained, brittle winter light broke through in intervals, landing upon the damp spot Theodora had chosen. Mist clung to the edges of the lilypond, the water gray and cold, the reeds around it wild and unloved.

She kept her gaze on the mist-soaked edges of the waterline, head turned towards the taller reeds, seeing nothing but the gray garden beyond, winter-bare and empty. Crows perched in the naked trees watched back, black eyes not fixed upon the still waters of the pond, but upon Theodora, their heads tilted down as if waiting.

"Six crows, Ottoline," Theodora said, pointing toward the stoic watchers. "Maybe we will find ourselves some gold."

"It is meant to be magpies, Miss Corvus," Ottoline said, not looking up from the book she was reading. "Not crows."

"They are all from the same family, though. Did you know that?"

Ottoline pressed a finger to the page, marking her spot. "Birds?"

Theodora bit her lip to stop her smile. "They are all a part of the corvid family, Ottoline. Crows, rooks, jackdaws, magpies."

"And yourself," Ottoline replied. "Are you not a crow?"

"Of a sort, Ottoline." Theodora pointed at the crows sitting silent above. "They have always fascinated me."

The young girl did not share Theodora's smile but looked up into the trees with her head cocked just like the birds watching her. "I think you miscounted."

"Oh, Ottoline." Theodora sighed, weary from her attempts at lifting the sullen girl's mood.

"Are they not all beggars and thieves?" Ottoline said, turning her page without reading it. "Unwanted mourners?"

"Not at all." Theodora took the book from Ottoline, setting it down on the damp grass. "They are clever and have been known to bestow gifts on those that treat them well. They don't forget kindness, Ottoline."

Ottoline looked to the house, at the deep shadows of Broken Oak. "Neither do I."

"My father," Theodora began, clasping the small hand of Ottoline. "Gave me the name Jackdora. Only he would call me that and it angered my grandmother greatly. I think she agreed with your views on crows, Ottoline, and that such a nickname was not becoming of a young woman like me."

Ottoline turned, eyes soft. "It suits you, Miss Corvus."

"Because I am a beggar and a thief?" Theodora laughed. Ottoline remained still, quiet.

"No," she said at last, fingers tightening around Theodora's. "Because I think you are a gift to us, Miss Corvus."

"That is a lovely thing to say, dear Ottoline." Theodora drew her close. "Do you have a nickname? One perhaps shared between you and your father?"

"Not one like yours, he calls me darling, or sweetheart. I do not have one that is only for me."

"Then we must find you one."

"What would you name me?" Ottoline pulled out of Theodora's hold, any softness in her face had slipped away.

"The farmyard down the lane from Woodrow House had an ill-tempered goose," Theodora began with a laugh. "How does little gosling sound?"

"I do not like it." No warmth lifted the girl's voice, no humor.

"Then we shall have to think more about it."

"I don't want the name of some farm animal, Miss Corvus."

"You are in a foul mood today, Ottoline," Theodora said, impatience seeping into her voice. "Whatever is the matter?"

"You said papa would be joining us today."

Theodora took in the gray skies and damp ground, her skirts already cold and slightly muddy. "Only if the sun was out, I fear it is too cold and damp for your father out here."

"Obviously you do not mind being damp and cold, Miss Corvus."

Theodora shrugged. "My skirts will dry, as will yours Ottoline."

"If you say so."

"I do say so," Theodora returned, tone firm. "I am sorry you are disappointed your father could not join us today, but it is a privilege to be able to take lessons outside. You will speak to me with the same respect I grant you, Ottoline, or do not speak at all."

She expected further sulking, the pouting of lips, the stamp of small feet pounding across the pathways while the echo of childish tears followed her into the house. Ottoline neither sulked, nor stomped, but she did weep. They were not the loud sobs of a spoiled child, but the quiet tears of someone whose heart was simply too full.

I care to see them, Theodora thought, knowing the hardship of hiding one's tears. *I care to see them, Ottoline.*

She pulled the child close, saying nothing about the tears, allowing them to fall upon her shoulder. As she wept, Theodora could feel the loosening of her small body against hers, the shuddering sigh as though she had held her breath for some time and was finally exhaling.

It did her good, Theodora could see that—feel that. It did her good for someone to see her weep.

While holding Ottoline tight to her chest, Theodora looked back up into the trees, to the crows that continued to watch. She counted the same six crows as before, no more and no less.

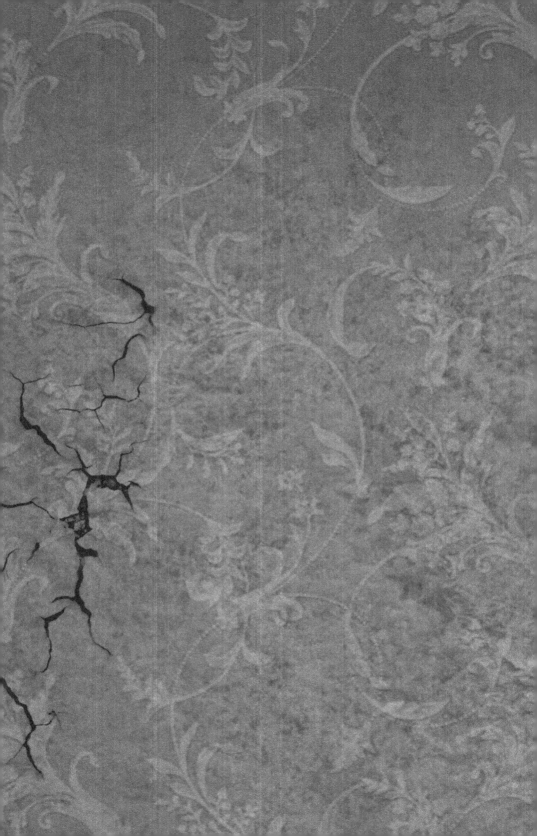

Eleven

Against reason

The evening brought with it more cloud and rain, the last burst of winter sunlight swallowed by the dense fog that drew in. No matter how close she sat to the fire, Theodora's skirts remained damp, the hems crusted with mud. Ms. Rivers had looked on in seething silence as she and Ottoline left a trail of filthy footprints upon her clean floors.

She sat, still enraged in her chair by the fireplace, her crochet hook digging into her work with wordless fury. Theodora had offered to mop the floors and been met with more stony silence.

"I am not here to clean up after you," she said finally, pointing her crochet hook in Theodora's direction. "You should know better than to gallivant around in the rain, Miss Corvus."

"Oh, come now, fresh air is good for the lungs," Theodora said, settling deeper into the chair opposite the housekeeper. "We will dry out and mud comes off floors. You should join us next time, Ms. Rivers."

The old housekeeper's brows rose so high, they near disappeared into her graying hair. "My days of dancing in the rain are long gone girl!"

"But you admit to dancing in it in your youth?"

The housekeeper pursed her lips, not quite disguising the smile pulling at its edges. "I will admit to nothing, Miss Corvus. Wipe your cursed feet next time you decide to run like a wildling in the rain."

Theodora stretched her legs before her, hoping the fire would at last warm her chilled bones. Her head rested upon the back of her chair, content. "Ottoline missed her father today," she said into the comfortable quiet.

"His lordship is affected by one of his headaches, I would have passed on the message sooner, but I am not chasing you around in the wet and cold, Miss Corvus."

Theodora sat up in concern. "He is unwell?"

"It will pass; it always does," the housekeeper said, not looking up from her crochet.

"May I look in on him?" Theodora asked, the quiet around her too stiff and close. "To see if he is in need of anything?"

"You doubt my words, Miss Corvus?" A tight-lipped smile pressed against the edges of Ms. Rivers's lips. "Go see for yourself, girl. You'll lend me no peace otherwise."

The hallways of Broken Oak were empty, the candles unlit. Moonlight slipped in through the gaps in the curtains, silvery light pooling upon the newly washed floors. Theodora needed no light to see, her feet recalling the winding corridors of the old house with ease.

She paused outside Ottoline's bedroom, listening for the sounds of movement, for any signs the girl would be out of bed to run wild in the darkness once more. Silence greeted her, heavy and calm. Satisfied that Ottoline was safely tucked in bed, Theodora took the last few steps to Cassias's room. She hovered a moment, thinking maybe she was intruding, stepping over some invisible barrier that she would not easily step back from.

She was deep in thought when the door opened.

"Dear me!" Cassias startled, eyes wide. "Theodora!"

"Ms. Rivers said you were ill," Theodora said quickly, stepping back to force more distance between them. "I wanted to check if I could assist in any way? How are you feeling? Can I get you anything?"

He said nothing for a moment, still looking quite baffled at her being outside his bedroom. "I am feeling much better, thank you," he said at last. "I was going to get some air."

Evening had slipped in cold and gloomy, the gray clouds darkening, bruise-like over the sky, each heavy with rain. Scant moonlight trickled down, catching the edges of the stone, the metal around the window frames. It bathed everything else in shadow.

"You can't possibly mean to go outside, Cassias?"

"Not quite." His smile deepened. "Would you care to join me? I would not object to company."

They walked together through the dark, standing close enough to touch. A breath existed between them, no more. Theodora followed through the kitchen, past the utility room and larder to a back door. It creaked when opened, a sharp noise in the quiet, leading out to an old glasshouse that half leaned against the side of the house.

"Not quite outside," Cassias said, gesturing for her to sit on one of the stone benches. Moss and lichen crept up the edges, spreading out from the cracks and crevices, veins of life in the cold stone.

"It looks as though it will fall down over our heads." Theodora stepped further into the glasshouse, looking up at the fragile looking beams, the iron brown with rust, a few of the window panes broken, allowing the brittle winter air to sweep in. Glass glinted from below the windows, as fine as sand.

"That it may." Cassias sat, tapping the space beside him. "Though I cannot remember a time when it did not look like this, and it has not fallen yet."

Theodora perched herself on the edge of the bench. "A miracle really." Her gaze fell upon the ivy clinging to the sidings, as though knitting it together, "I sometimes wonder if these old houses stand tall out of spite. I know Woodrow should have crumbled to dust a long time ago."

"I like the idea of that," Cassias said, leaning forward with his arms on his knees. "To refuse to fall into ruin, as though it is a choice to be made."

The air around them, though cold, held none of the bite of the wind outside. It was a bearable chill, almost comfortable.

"Ottoline missed you today." Her voice thrummed around the glasshouse.

"I was not myself," Cassias answered, sitting back up. "I sometimes feel the cold soak into my bones, a weight seems to fall on me, pressing me down, pressing my head down until I cannot think straight."

Theodora gave him a goodhearted nudge. "Perhaps it is you that should have taken to the seaside, Cassias."

He blinked up at her, brown eyes almost black in the low light. "The seaside?"

"In place of your wife."

He nodded then, slow and deliberate. "Yes, I suppose so."

They listened together to the sound of rain on the glass, to the scrape of bare branches over the roof. It was a place of in betweens, and Theodora found she liked it. Not quite inside or out, with the sound of the night close overhead. She could see why Cassias liked it; it was a good place to simply be.

At her side, she could feel the weight of Cassias press against her, his head slowly beginning to loll upon her shoulder. With care and softness, Theodora placed her hand on his arm. "You look tired still and it is growing darker and colder here. Shall we go back?"

Cassias blinked, straightening himself with a cough. "I think that would be best." He took her hand and stood, and with an elegant nod of his head he pulled Theodora to her feet. "I am really not myself, and for that I must apologize."

"There is no need," Theodora said, noting his hand still lingered on hers. She withdrew it gently. "It was myself, after all, that came calling at your door knowing you were unwell. Are you feeling any better?"

"A little weary, that is all." Cassias took a small step back, seeming to notice, as Theodora had done, the closeness between them. "Thank you for your company this evening, Theodora."

"Thank you for showing me this…" she paused, looking up at the cracked glass, the dried roots dangling from the beams, the thick webbing in the corners. "This unique spot of yours."

His laughter echoed. "You wound me, Theodora." Cassias placed a hand to his heart, his sudden smile wide and wonderful.

"Not too deeply, I hope?"

"No, not too deeply."

Leaving the crooked glasshouse behind, they walked back through the corridors of Broken Oak. They passed the sitting room in darkness, the candles snuffed out, the embers in the fire glowing faintly. Theodora left Cassias outside his bedroom, pausing to listen at Ottoline's door. No sound came from within, so she bid him goodnight and climbed the narrow stairs and corridors to her own little room above them all.

Despite the generous fire in her room, the chill in Theodora's bones remained. She bundled the blankets tight around her, yet could not get warm. She knew with little doubt she would wake with a cold, and it would serve her right for playing out in the rain that afternoon. She only hoped that Ottoline would not get sick, though the child had seemed in good health when she tucked her in for the night.

Theodora slipped gently into sleep, lulled by the soft rainfall at the window—only to be awoken sometime later by footsteps outside her door.

"Ottoline!" she shouted in the darkness, irritated from being drawn from the sleep and warmth that had finally laid claim to her. "This is getting ridiculous."

Theodora rose from the bed and wrenched her bedroom door open to peer into the nothingness outside the room.

Footsteps echoed upon the floor as a flash of white vanished around the corner. Theodora followed, quick and quiet, her footfalls silent. She walked down the hallway, hand against the wall, to the staircase leading up into the old servant quarters.

Theodora paused and listened for the soft shuffle of footsteps. She would catch the girl out of bed if she had to traipse across the house to do so.

"Ottoline!" The word was an angry hiss. "I truly have had enough of this nonsense. There will be no further treats and no more lessons by the pond—that I can assure you."

She quickened her pace along the cold, forgotten passageway above her room, the way ahead soaked in darkness. She called for the girl again, and her voice did not echo back. The house, in its eternal silence, held still; the beams overhead, old as they were, creaked not.

Speak to me.

Theodora stepped further into the shadows, using the scant slice of moonlight to find her way. There were no footsteps, no sounds. She made to turn back, away from the stark darkness of the corridor and the attic door with its gleaming doorknob. The air around her shifted, tightened, like a breath held. Within the dark, against the quiet, she remained, turning in time to see the drift of white just before her.

Closer she moved, closer and closer, hand outstretched to clasp the arm of someone who was definitely not Ottoline.

"Lord Thorne?" Theodora grasped his arm harder. "Cassias, what in heaven's name are you doing?"

He turned slowly, standing before her in only his shirtsleeves. His hand came up to touch hers, long fingers curling tightly. Though he looked directly at her, Theodora knew he was not seeing her at all.

"Where are you going?" she asked softly, trying and failing to catch his gaze.

He stared, unblinking, words slow and strange. "I cannot find her."

"Who?"

He tugged at her hand, nails digging into the soft skin of her palm. "Where is she?"

"Come," Theodora said, coaxing him away from the attic with a gentle hand. "There is no one up here save you and I."

He moved beside her with an odd gait, not quite leaning upon her, but absolutely not standing of his own accord.

It had scarcely been a few hours since she had left him at his door. "Cassias, are you drunk?"

He did not answer but turned to stare back down into the darkness, hand pulling away from Theodora's. "I need to find her..." The words slurred and slipped from his mouth, his free hand coming up to press against the side of his head.

Theodora shifted to stand in front of him, bending low so she could meet his eyes. He looked up from his slouched position, squinting back at her.

"Can you hear her?"

"I can hear nothing but the drunken ramblings of a man who ought to be in his bed, as I ought to be in mine, Cassias."

With a firm grip, she clasped the young lord's elbow, near dragging him through the shadows and down the flights of stairs, away from the old servant floor. He came with relative ease, loose-limbed and hopeless.

"Ms. Rivers said you were ill and that is why you could not join Ottoline and myself today," Theodora said, not looking back. "You said you were ill. I can see now that your ailment was self-inflicted, and I cannot lend you any sympathy."

"Ottoline?"

"Yes, Lord Thorne, Ottoline." The words ground out from behind her teeth, her entire self fed up with the late-night wanderings of half the household. "She wept today, tears for a father that would rather see the bottom of a liquor bottle than his own daughter."

The words tumbled too quick and too harsh from her mouth, and it was with some relief that Theodora thought her employer too drunk to remember them come morning.

"Ottoline," he repeated, the word not quite a question, not quite anything.

Cassias tore his arm from Theodora's unforgiving hold and wove his way across the landings and corridors of Broken Oak Manor, one hand against the walls to steady himself. Theodora could only follow him.

Despite his inebriated state, Cassias seemed to know the twists and turns of Broken Oak without fault. His footsteps, though clumsy, did not pause, did not rest. With one hand ever against the wall, he led Theodora to a landing she knew well.

He stopped outside Ottoline's bedroom, hand hesitant upon the doorknob. He swayed, and Theodora caught his arm. With a finger placed at her lips, she turned the knob and pushed it open. She followed him as he stepped inside, remaining close to the door. Cassias took three long strides to the girl sleeping in the bed, small body tucked under the covers Theodora had secured her under. Cassias slipped to his knees in silence, head resting against the pillow his daughter slumbered upon.

There he remained, silent, arm outstretched, fingers clutched around the blanket. He kept his head bowed, shoulders trembling. With great care, Theodora reached for him, hand barely touching his shoulder.

"You'll wake her," she whispered, voice a breath. "Come, let's get you to bed."

He rose, moving with a grace he had not possessed moments before. He still leaned against her, accepting the arm she placed around his without question. With little fuss, she led him from Ottoline's bedroom, down the moonlight-flooded corridor, to his own chambers.

Theodora guided him into his room, keeping hold of his arm while she took in the shadowed space. The walls were papered in deep blue with flowers of the richest hues and exotic birds painted on them. The high windows boasted layers of velvet and silks, draping to the floor in pools of opulence.

The near-darkness folded around his bed, around the tall bed posts with their golden spiked tops. It wove around the headboard, all carved tendrils of vines and roses. It was everywhere, that darkness—it clung to the cooling embers of the fireplace, dripping from the blackened wicks of unlit candles.

"Ms. Rivers will light them come morning," Cassias murmured, staggering the last few steps to his bed.

Theodora wrapped her arms around herself. "Are you not cold?"

"Tired," he replied. "Just tired."

Cassias crawled beneath the heavy coverlets, the velvets and silks, dark hair spilling out over the pillows. Theodora knew she should not linger—that propriety insisted she turn and leave him to the shadows. But there, in that heavy darkness, she stayed a moment, waiting until he had slipped into the kind of sleep one did not easily wake from.

"You will feel the consequences of this come morning," she whispered, shaking her head. "Do not think I will be putting you to bed again, you foolish man."

He lay unmoving with his head on the silk pillows. Moonlight crept through the gap in the curtains, settling with care across his face. He looked peaceful, at least, still eyelids framed by lashes blacker than soot.

Theodora left him to his slumber, telling herself she had lingered only to ensure he would not go wandering again. She did not stay to admire the way his lip turned up slightly as he slept, did not stay to take in the sharpness of his cheekbones, the line of his jaw, did not stay to watch his hand curl around the edge of the bed, long fingers stretching as they had over her own hand.

No. She stayed to ensure he did not wander, and that was all.

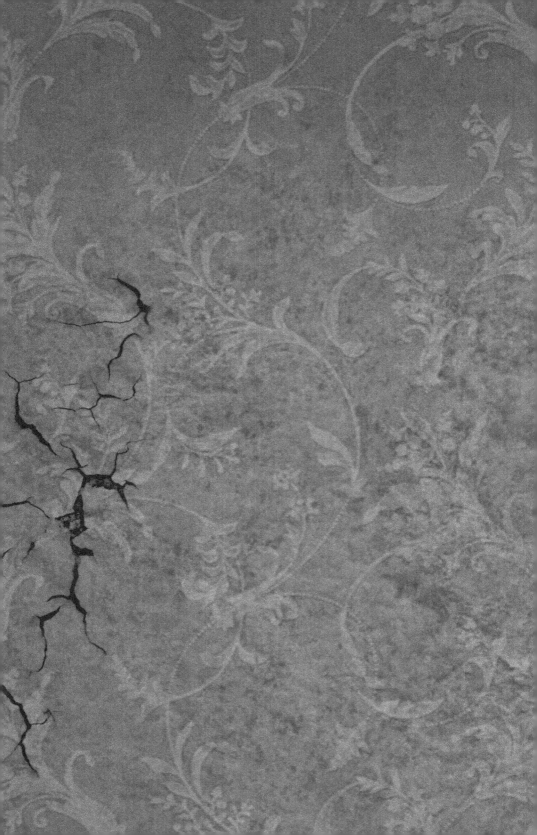

Twelve

Whatever walked there

The fires were made up full and hearty when Theodora went down the next morning. The candles were all lit too, placed in the corners where the shadows liked to gather. The house was bathed in a welcoming glow, the chill outside banished while the fires burned.

"I will keep them hot, Miss Corvus," Ms. River said, tea in hand. "The cold air does nothing for his Lordship's headaches."

"Hmm, neither does a bottle of brandy." Theodora settled down at the table beside the old housekeeper. "If it is not Ottoline I am chasing around the landings, it is the lord of the manor himself."

Ms. Rivers heaped a generous spoonful of sugar into her tea, watching Theodora over the rim of the cup. Steam rose, fragrant and familiar, filling the air where words would not. "The cold does…"

"Please do not make excuses for him, Ms. Rivers. I am not naïve enough to mistake a man deep in his cups for someone who has a chill, at least not for a second time!"

"Speaking of chills, I do so hope your skirts dried out from the other day, it would be an awful shame if you fell ill."

Theodora ran a hand down her dress to the dark stains that marred the hem and would not come out. "They still feel damp, Ms. Rivers. Would you be so kind as to stoke up the fire in my room, so I could perhaps dry out fully?"

"I shall add it to the never-ending list of things I am to do to keep this house going." The old housekeeper returned her cup to its saucer, the tea untouched. "Lest it fall to ruin around me."

There was no anger in the woman's tone, just resignation that, no matter how hard she might try to keep everything in order, the house was simply too large for her alone to maintain. Theodora thought back to Woodrow House, to its slow decay and reluctance to fall completely to ruin. Her grandmother would die in that house, surrounded by the creeping rot, her every rasping breath taking on more and more of the house's demise as she waited for her own. Then, she supposed, it would be Theodora's. An empty ruin left absent by the ghosts who refused to haunt it.

She wondered whether Ms. Rivers would stay at Broken Oak, whether she would watch on as time took pieces of the grand house until slowly, ever so slowly, the decay made it brittle, and it bled its secrets. She wondered what it would say, that quiet house, when at last it fell.

"May I ask how long you have worked here at Broken Oak, Ms. Rivers?"

"Too long, it seems," the housekeeper answered with a sigh. "I am older than I look, but the work keeps me young. I keep it well, don't you think, despite the circumstances."

"Of there being no other staff?"

"That too."

"I honestly do not know how you do it all, my grandmother would have loved to have you as part of her household."

"Respectfully, Miss Corvus, your ancestral home has been falling into disrepair for some time, I feel it may be too much even for my hands."

"That is a fair observation," Theodora said. "There truly is no hope for it."

Ms. Rivers said nothing for a time, tapping her fingers on the side of her teacup. She did not look up when at last she said, "With it being Sunday, Miss Corvus, your time is yours to do with as you please."

Theodora noted the prompt, but her good manners would not allow her to simply get up at leave. "I can help you with any jobs, if you can find use for me?"

"The offer is appreciated, but you will only get beneath my feet," the housekeeper replied with a dismissive wave.

So, with the day stretching out in front of her, Theodora left the warmth of the kitchen and went in search of something to occupy herself with.

Often, Theodora felt at a loss having free time. Though there were days at Woodrow where she would wander the house, alone and quiet, it was not time given to her. At Kingsward, she had been allowed to have her little room with her little table and little chair, yet it always felt as though she were waiting, sitting primly before being called up to the dark, overbearing library with its unread books and a lord with heavy hands.

The time at Broken Oak felt different. That for the first time, it truly was hers to enjoy. There were the grounds to explore, the other side of the pond where the reeds grew taller, the small pockets of garden left barren over the winter. Her feet itched to see it all, to imprint Broken Oak into her memory as thoroughly as she had Woodrow.

Theodora did not venture out into the gardens on her first

morning off, despite the weather clearing, instead making her way upstairs to where Ottoline played.

Watery sunlight fell upon the floor, catching the dust motes dancing in the air. Ottoline sat with her back to the door, dress spilled out around her. At hearing the latch of the door, she turned, eyes narrowed.

"Are you here for extra lessons, Miss Corvus?" she asked, wary.

Theodora stepped into the room and settled herself beside Ottoline. She marveled at the beautiful details carved on the bedposts and the drawers, seeing how perfect it was, how it had been created with love.

"Not to worry, dear Ottoline," Theodora answered with a laugh. "The day is yours. I thought I would just pop my head in to see what plans you had and to tell you I am always close by, if you need me."

Leaning forward, Theodora could see the little scraps of paper Ottoline held in her lap, all torn from the pages of her artbook. Long dried paint-colored edges, the images ruined. Ottoline caught Theodora's gaze and held it.

"No one will miss these paintings, Miss Corvus," she explained with a wry smile. "My stepmother was ever so critical of them."

"She taught you to paint?"

Ottoline shrugged. "She taught me to dislike it."

Theodora plucked up one of the pieces of paper and turned it over. There, in small, neat handwriting were the words:

To take a picnic down by the river near the church.

She took another while Ottoline watched on in silence.

Go horse riding on Old Jack.

Another and Another...

Go for tea at the Singing Teapot. Dance around the maypole at the spring fair

Ottoline's lap was filled with them, scraps of her unwanted art made into wishes. Her small hands fumbled with them, searching through each wish before she passed one to Theodora.

To ride the carousel with Miss Corvus and Papa.

An ache lay heavy on Theodora's tear-stained heart, one of hope and wanting. "Have you a jar to put these in, Ottoline? To keep them safe."

Theodora waited while Ottoline went in search of a suitable container, her hands passing over empty jam jars filled with paint brushes, and little cardboard boxes with silk ribbons. She returned to the middle of the room with a black music box, small white moths painted on its sides, taking flight amongst a galaxy of tiny stars.

"I want to keep them in here," Ottoline said, lifting the lid. Inside, a ballet dancer began to slowly spin to the sweet tinkling of a lullaby.

"A perfect place." Theodora folded the wish in her hand and settled it amongst all the others. With a smile she turned the key and placed the box between them. "We will have to see how many of these wishes we can make come true."

The music played out over Ottoline's room, filling the space with a sense of wonder and magic, in a way only a child's toy could. Theodora turned the key again when the music stopped, humming along to the lullaby she remembered from when she was a little girl, one her father had shared with her. It was a song of comfort, one of love, of goodnight kisses and soft lamplight. She turned the key a third time, not quite ready to leave the memory of her father. The lullaby began, then halted as though cut off, quick and jarring. The ballerina stood frozen, caught mid-twirl in the sudden silence.

Ottoline looked on, and without a word, carefully closed the lid.

"Is it broken?" Theodora asked, reaching to check the little brass key.

Ottoline shrugged. "Only sometimes."

"Perhaps it can be fixed, would you like me to take a look? I fixed one of our old clocks once, this may be not so different."

Ottoline shook her head, rising to place the music box back on its shelf. "It belonged to my mother."

"I would be very careful with it."

"I believe you would be, Miss Corvus." Ottoline smoothed the folds of her dress, rosebud lips curving into a gentle smile. "Tell me what else you have planned for your day off?"

Theodora noted the change of subject, eyes flicking to the music box sitting silent nearby. "I have not yet decided."

"The library is always rather lovely this time of day."

"Then I shall venture there," Theodora replied with a smile, sensing the dismissal from her young charge. "You will know where to find me."

Theodora found her way to Broken Oak's library, the smell of old books and worn leather swooping over her in an embrace. It was not the crowded, dark space of Kingsward Manor's—the bookcases so unlike the walls of that labyrinthine library with its rough hands and filthy whispers. It stood open and bright with tall windows allowing winter sunlight to pour through, so there was hardly a need for the candlelight at all. It yawned open, a sleepy room of lazy sunlight and slow shadows. Rugs adorned the polished floors, fat chairs nestled within alcoves beside reading tables, in front of windows overlooking the barren gardens. Winding iron staircases led to high above, the railings heavy with scrollwork. They led to more books, more knowledge than any one person could consume in a lifetime.

Theodora was half settled in a comfortable armchair, allowing the day to simply wash over her, to pass without the need to do anything. Her gaze was fixed on the view of the sweeping lawns and mist-covered pond, quiet and content in her solitude, when Cassias stepped in.

"I was not expecting to see you up quite so early," Theodora said, not turning from the window.

Cassias hovered a moment before claiming the chair opposite hers. "May I inquire as to why?"

She looked at him, dressed in his good clothes with the ruby at his neck. The loose curls of his hair brushed over his shoulders, neat and no longer wild. No shadows lingered beneath his dark eyes.

"I found you wandering the halls last night."

A shocked laugh slipped from his lips. "That is absurd."

"What was absurd, Cassias, was finding you in little more than a crumpled shirt."

Cassias ran a hand over his immaculate clothes, the well-tailored trousers, the perfect jacket that had literally been made just for him. He seemed to take offense that he had been caught looking rumpled, rather than the fact he had been caught out at all.

"I..." He paused a moment, confusion softening the sharp edges of his face. "Are you quite sure it was me?"

Words failed Theodora, and she took a moment to fix the incredulous look she knew was upon her face. "Who else could it have been? Cassias, I had to help you find your way to your bed."

He looked as mortified as she felt. The words tumbled from his lips, quick and uncomfortable. "I don't remember...I can't think... You were in my bedroom?"

"Out of necessity!" She ensured the statement was clear—that she most certainly did not find herself putting grown men to bed on a regular basis.

"Heavens!"

"You could barely stand..."

"Undressed?"

She could not meet his eyes. "Somewhat."

Cassias leaned forward, resting his head on clasped hands. "You put me to bed?"

Theodora nodded, before realizing he could not see her. "You did manage to find the bed independently."

He groaned into his hands.

"You were quite distressed. How much did you drink last night?"

"I didn't—"

"Cassias." Theodora reached out, only just stopping herself from placing it upon his knee. She recalled the feel of his fingers around her own, the weight of him against her body.

"I have no memory of last night," he admitted, looking up. His eyes fixed upon her hand, as though, through the darkness of his memories, he recalled her touch. "I do not know what came over me."

"You were looking for someone." Theodora drew her hands back into her lap, sitting straighter to secure more distance between them. "Perhaps your wife?"

"My wife?"

Loneliness could be cruel, Theodora understood that. So often, she had wandered the rotting floorboards of Woodrow House in need of a friend, a kind word, a smile. Her grandmother had never been quite enough, the servants around her not enough. She recalled when her father lived—for a short time, for a wondrous time, she had not felt so alone.

Theodora did not wish for anyone to be alone. "It is understandable that you miss her."

"Perhaps." Cassias swept a hand through his hair, disturbing the curls. "I cannot tell you how sorry I am for what happened last night, Theodora. I don't make a habit of wandering the halls at night out of my senses, I assure you. Please, I beg of you, forgive me and never mention it again."

"I promise I shall never again bring up the night of you and your shirtsleeves, Lord Thorne."

He threw her a cutting look. "You are teasing me, again."

A smile tugged at the edges of Theodora's lips. "Only a little, and only this once."

His own smile was a gentle thing. "I don't believe you in the slightest."

The winter sunlight slowly turned to rain, clouds coming in low and heavy and dark. It pattered against the window panes, the sound soothing. The library darkened with it, but it was a tender darkness. They sat in the soft shadows, relaxed and content.

"It is hard to imagine spring unfolding from the clutches of winter on days like these," Cassias said, head resting against the back of his armchair. "It feels as though everything is paused and waiting."

"At Woodrow, the winter would sink its teeth in and take more of the house by the time spring wound in." Theodora kept her gaze upon the garden with its bare trees and mist-heavy pond. "We would go searching, my father and I, in the gardens for snowdrops or the stubborn headed stalks of early daffodils. When we found one, we would dig it up with care and plant it in a pot to bring inside, where it would finally bloom. The first bud of spring, flowering within the house that winter could not take."

"Do you think anything is unfurling out there?"

"Maybe." Theodora thought of the roses slumbering deep, to the dried husks of seed heads that had scattered into the dormant beds. There was promise to that little patch of garden, no matter how sparse and sickly it appeared.

The house kept silent as night fell and the dark grew solid and cold. No noise woke Theodora, no footsteps echoed beyond her door, beckoning her to follow. She slept soundly until the damp chill of morning.

It was the cold that woke her, the chill of frost and early rain. The fire lay unlit, the coals nothing but white ash that had spilled from the grate to settle on the floor. Theodora sat up, eyes lingering upon the cold white dust from the fireplace—then to the muddied footprints across her floorboards.

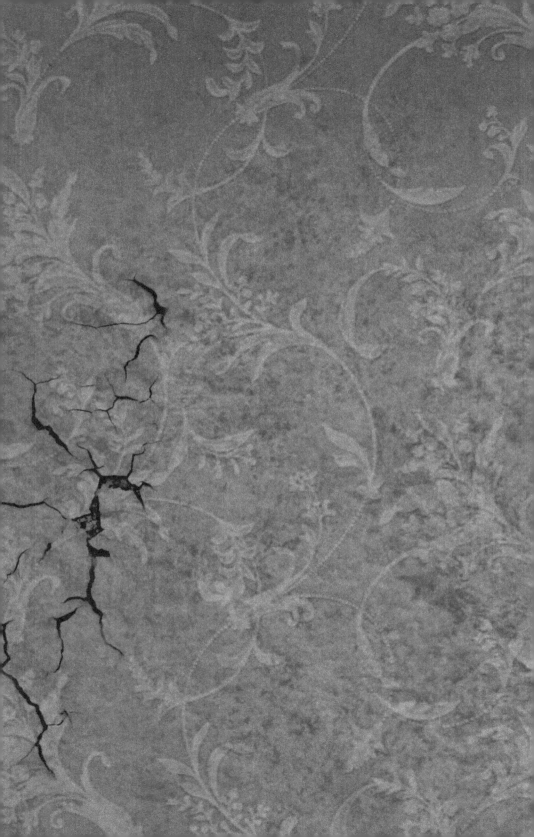

Thirteen

For those who listen

The piano spilled out the tune to an old waltz that Theodora had nearly forgotten; a song that she had once danced to when the ballroom at Woodrow House was made for dancing and the floors had yet to sink into its foundations.

Ottoline's fingers stumbled over a few notes, slow and determined, as Theodora thought back to the lavish balls her grandmother would host, the people who filled the halls, the laughter and the music. It seemed to matter little that the house did not stand as firm as other grand houses—that it was allowed to show its age, its groaning limbs to those decorated in masks and finery. Woodrow had once worn its decrepit bones with a strange sort of elegance, one the gentry had taken pleasure dancing within.

Theodora's grandmother would have her dressed in her finest gown, made for her that season by the best seamstress, despite her father's protests that they were a waste of good money. She would wear them only once, the silks decadent and soft, the skirts full, before they were put away to be forgotten about by all but the ever-hungry moths.

There were never any other children, and Theodora would feel quite like a cherished porcelain doll, pretty and expensive. Quiet.

Her father would dance with her and no one else, balancing her small shoes upon his larger ones as they waltzed across the room, uncaring of Grandmother's disapproving gaze. She remembered his smile, the laughter in his eyes, quick at his lips. It was the only time he would smile when beneath the eaves of Woodrow House, when Theodora was in his arms, as the waltz played on.

"Shall I play another?"

Theodora blinked, the memory scattering like dust motes in the sunlight. "Would you play that once again, Ottoline?"

"I keep forgetting the notes, Miss Corvus."

"All the better to play it again and again," she said, closing her eyes as Ottoline's small hands swept along the keys, this time a little faster, the song taking root within the heavy part of Theodora's chest.

Theodora did not hear the door slip open, nor the approaching footsteps, too lost within the stumbling music to pay heed to anything else.

"I keep making mistakes," Ottoline huffed, frustrated hands clashing against the keys. "I fear I will be learning this song for eternity and still not perfect it."

A shadow loomed over Theodora, and she glanced up at last.

Cassias stood close, eyes focused on the music sheet. "I know this song," he said, arm brushing Theodora as he splayed his fingers over the keys. He caught her eye, and shifted so they were no longer touching. "Here, Ottoline, like this."

He played the notes slowly, fingers brushing the keys with a gentleness that captivated Theodora. He turned to her, smiling. So close. Too close. He paused, fingers hovering over the last key.

"Apologies, Miss Corvus," he said, voice faltering as he withdrew. "I did not mean to trespass."

"Not at all." Her voice was quiet, unsure. Her mind was filled with the music, her senses filled with the scent of him—a strange sweetness and the dust of old houses. "Please, play on."

It would have been easy to move, to shift aside so he could sit beside Ottoline. But she remained, seated upon the piano stool with him above her, his presence solid at her back.

Ottoline began again, small fingers determined to press the correct keys. Cassias held her hand, guiding her with such care, such tenderness, repeating the same few notes over and over. They played together, hands echoing over the song, slow and staggering, but it was beautiful.

They stumbled together, Ottoline's face scrunched with concentration, Cassias' alight with patience and wonder. He did not scold, nor berate, but took her hand, squeezed lightly and began again.

Theodora was lost in the moment, the softness of it, the gentle joy. It reminded her of the days spent with her own father, of a time when her chest was not heavy, her heart not a weight, too full and aching. Without thinking, she reached out, joining the halting melody with her own.

And so, they played, the strange song a mix of flawless notes and missed keys.

That evening, long after Ottoline had been tucked into bed and the night drew in dark and cold, Theodora found herself in the sitting room, settled by the fire with Ms. Rivers and Cassias.

Ms. Rivers had set aside her crochet to sit at the piano, her fingers gliding along the keys with a familiarity Ottoline did not yet possess. The music filled the room in a way the candlelight could not, bringing a warmth that settled in Theodora's bones.

Cassias sat in his armchair, feet up on a footstool, a soft smile at his mouth. "It seems like you have not played in forever, Ms. Rivers. I have so missed the sound."

"I worried I would forget how to play," Ms. Rivers said, the tune at her fingers sweet and gentle. "It is too easy to forget if we sit idle—forget who we are and who will be if we think, for a moment, we can stop moving."

"Is that why you keep so busy?" Theodora asked. "To remember?"

"I am an old woman, Miss Corvus, I must allow my mind to remember lest my spirit forget. What use could I be to the house then?"

"We would find use for you, Ms. Rivers," Cassias said, smile widening. "Fear not."

"I do fear what this house will become without me, boy. You do not know how to keep it."

Cassias chuckled, uncaring at how the old housekeeper addressed him. "That is the truth."

"Surely you know something about running a house, Cassias?" Theodora laughed, knowing a dwelling such as Broken Oak could not remain standing with no one looking out for it.

"I have books and mountains of paperwork to say you are right, Theodora. I have one or two certificates to imply I have some knowledge. I know that this sprawling tower of stone will one day fall to my daughter, who will likely hate it as much as I do."

Ms. Rivers's tune changed, the lightness of the melody deepening. "Then why not leave, Your Lordship?"

The laughter slipped away. "You know I cannot."

"Why?"

Cassias paused, head tilting to gaze up at the ceiling, past the elaborate swirls and moldings, past the gold leaf, to somewhere far above. "It is my home."

"Indeed."

The music ceased, the room settling into echoes and then silence. No one spoke into it, that quiet, so it loomed around them, heavy and unwanted.

"May I request a song?" Theodora asked at last, words breaking through the discomfort. Ms. Rivers gave a quick nod, not turning from the piano. "This is one of my favorites."

The song at Ms. Rivers's hands once more took hold of Theodora's heart—the waltz flowing perfect and wonderful, as flawless as the times it had played at Woodrow House. Ms. Rivers played without faltering, her fingers finding the notes like old friends. Theodora hoped the melody would seep into the cold stone of Broken Oak and settle there beside its secrets, slipping out in times of need.

Cassias held a hand out to her, words gentle against the quick notes of the waltz. "Dance with me?"

She hesitated, the memory of his closeness the night before still fresh—the feel of his fingers, his shoulder against hers. She thought of his closeness earlier that day, the brush of his arm. They had sat at the same piano just hours before, played the same song, allowing the music to call them closer. Theodora thought of the cold stare of Cassias's wife, the painted firmness of her lips, how she would feel at Theodora's hand holding that of her husband.

"Please." The word fell from his lips, a breath and little more.

Theodora took his hand, allowing him to pull her to her feet. He smiled down at her from beneath dark lashes, one hand gently settling above her hip, the other firmly holding her own.

They moved together with practiced grace, feet gliding to the steps they both knew by heart. Ms. Rivers played on, the melody awakening a long-buried piece of Theodora.

The hand at her waist tightened, fingers splayed over the fabric of her skirts. They shared space and breath, bodies joined by music. She dared look up, aware they were too close. Cassias met her gaze, dark eyes serious. The smile had slipped, his lips hinting at a frown. But his hands remained firm upon her—firmer than they needed to be.

"I cannot help but wonder if you are judging my dancing, Lord Thorne? I have not yet stepped upon your toes."

Cassias blinked as though coming back to himself. "You dance beautifully, Theodora. Forgive me, my mind went elsewhere."

Theodora could guess where his thoughts perhaps wandered,

even Ms. Rivers glanced around from the keys to lift an eyebrow at the young lord. "We do not have to dance, Cassias, if you would like to stop."

"I think it would be wise." But there he remained, hand against her waist, fingers curled around hers.

"You have to let me go."

He nodded and pulled his hands back, hiding them in his pockets as though he feared they might reach out again. "Goodnight, Theodora."

"Goodnight, Cassias." She curtsied, a dip of her knees, a bob of her skirts, and he inclined his head, dark hair falling across his eyes.

She watched him leave the room, tall frame bent over slightly as if adjusting to a weight carried that lay, like Theodora's, hidden.

Ms. Rivers was looking at Theodora when she turned back around, hands in her lap, the last echoes of her song fading into the walls.

"You look at me as though I have done something wrong," Theodora said, voice quiet. "Somehow, I feel as though I have done wrong."

"I cannot say that you have or have not, girl," the housekeeper said with a sigh. "Only that I said for you to take care and I fear you are not."

"It is a lonely house." Theodora turned to the empty doorway, words slipping through to follow into the shadows. "Is it so terrible not to wish to be alone?"

"Take care, girl," Ms. Rivers repeated. "You are to be here a while and, no matter how big and how lonely this house may be, haunting its corridors with a broken heart will make it appear lonelier still."

"We are friends, Ms. Rivers," Theodora said, still looking toward the darkness, listening for footfalls. There was nothing but silence waiting in the shadows. "Simply friends and nothing more, I assure you."

The housekeeper lifted her chin, nodding to the doorway. "Indeed, Miss Corvus."

"May I sit with you a while, Ms. Rivers?"

The housekeeper ran her fingers over the keys of the piano, teasing out another song. "I will not object to your company."

Theodora sat in the armchair Cassias had vacated close to the fire. She listened to the old housekeeper play, allowing the music to sweep over her and take her away.

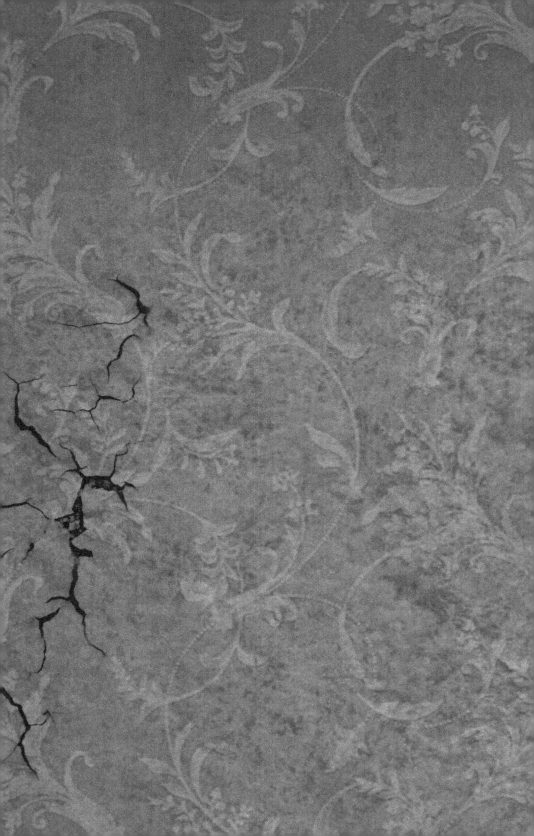

Fourteen

༄

The grief that does not speak

Screams awoke Theodora, shrill cries of fear that had her running down the corridors. They echoed, those cries, along the walls, the empty hallways, beckoning her on and on and on. Faster and faster. Quick! They urged her. Come quick!

Theodora came to a stop before Ottoline's room, the cries echoing from within. She spared a fleeting glance down the landing, to where Cassias slept undisturbed by his daughter's anguished shouts.

With a scowl at his door, she rushed into Ottoline's room and to her bedside, taking the small girl into her arms. A small gasp escaped Ottoline's lips, her body, for just a moment, going stiff. The screams resided, and she began to weep. She remained there a while, holding her close, whispering gently until the sobs softened into silent tears. Theodora cared to see them, cared to feel them soak deeply through the fabric of her clothing, cared enough to allow them to seep through into her tear-hardened heart so they would not weigh upon Ottoline's.

"Was it a nightmare, dear Ottoline?" she asked, one hand lifting to the girl's cheeks to wipe away the remaining tears.

"No, Miss Corvus."

"Then what has frightened you?"

Ottoline only turned to peer into the shadows over Theodora's shoulder. She followed the girl's gaze into the shadows, to watch as the moonlight caught the dust motes and cast its gentle light upon the rockers of the rocking chair. She finally heard it then—the tap, tap, tapping of the chair rocking back and forth.

The unloved doll, Juliet, stared back from the shadows, painted eyes blank as she rocked in the chair, back and forth, back and forth, back and forth, with not a soul touching it.

"Come, Ottoline." Theodora scooped the girl into her arms, holding her tight as she fled the room, the tapping growing fainter and fainter, until they could not hear it at all.

She raced down the winding corridors, the girl tight in her arms, nothing but silence behind them. Ottoline clung to her, limpet tight, head buried against her shoulder. She did not stop until they reached her bedroom, thankful for the glow of the candlelight and the crackle of the fire. It filled the room with light and warmth, a welcoming glow after the creaking darkness they had fled from. Theodora set Ottoline down on the edge of the bed, turning to close the door behind them.

"I can stay with you, Miss Corvus?" Ottoline asked, hands brushing over the harsh blankets of Theodora's bed. If she missed the velvets and silks of her own chambers, she did not say.

Theodora nodded, tucking her in tightly. "For tonight, Ottoline."

"I told you Juliet was naughty, that is why I put her away." Ottoline looked up, eyes wide and wet.

"Perhaps Ms. Rivers moved her when tidying up," Theodora said, wiping the tears from Ottoline's cheeks. "A fine doll such as Juliet really ought not be shoved in the toybox."

"I'm frightened," Ottoline whispered into the dark. "I am so very frightened, Miss Corvus."

"It was only the wind," Theodora replied, slipping beneath the blankets and settling down beside the small girl. "The wind and nothing more."

"Then why did you flee?"

"I thought it best for you to settle with me, rather than spend half the night fearful and awake." The lie came with ease, the words a comfort to the girl tangled in her bedsheets. As sleep swept over Ottoline, peaceful and gentle, Theodora looked toward her bedroom door, as though she could see down through the walls and stairways to the room below. She knew that Ottoline's window had been closed.

After morning lessons, Theodora took Ottoline by the hand and led her to the damp grounds beside the lilypond, stretching out on the grass with a sigh. A sprawling willow tree stood nearby, long tendrils sweeping the water's edge, disturbing the calm.

"It looks as though we may escape the rain today, Ottoline. Why don't you see if you can spot some frogspawn? We could collect them in a jar."

A wide grin stretched across the young girl's face. "Father does hate frogs."

"Then you do not have to show him."

"Oh, but I must!" Ottoline picked up her skirts and darted toward the edge. "He will be horrified!"

"Go careful, you don't wish to fall in. Ms. Rivers will have a fit if I have to drag you back sopping wet." Theodora laughed, content.

She sat on the embankment, watching the water lap toward the earth, so dark she could not see its depths. More trees threw their winter-stripped shadows over the pond—all white limbs and thin branches. Crows watched from the boughs with cold disinterest, black eyes unblinking and uncaring. They clicked their beaks, caws echoing across the late morning, shattering the calm, the quiet. Theodora could not shake the feeling that they were mocking her.

"There is no frogspawn here," Ottoline said, slumping back onto the grass with great disappointment. "I wanted to chase him with it."

"I believe it may be too early for frogspawn, dear Ottoline," Theodora said, taking the girl's cold, wet hands. "Though I do think I should put a stop to you tormenting your poor father."

"Tormenting me with what, Miss Corvus?"

Theodora turned, startled to see Cassias Thorne standing above her. The wind caught his dark curls, sweeping them back from his face. His hands were in his pockets, brown eyes looking out to the pond where his daughter had played.

"I was wondering whether to stop Ottoline from chasing you with frogspawn come spring."

His gaze dipped to hers, one slender brow lifting. "What did you decide?"

"I hadn't, not yet."

"And here I was, thinking we were friends." He placed a hand to his heart. "Such cruelty from a young woman, Theodora."

She smiled back up at him. "Such cowardice from a gentleman, Cassias."

Cassias Thorne outstretched a hand to her, fingers folding over hers as she took it. He pulled her to her feet, the skirts around her ankles wet and muddied. For a moment, for longer than a moment, they simply stood there.

"I wonder what the weather is like at the coast," Theodora began, drawing her hand away, "I imagine the sea air is wonderful, a tonic for the soul."

"I have no doubts," Cassias replied, glancing back at the house, all shadows and darkness. "Maybe it is too good."

Theodora followed his gaze to the countless windows of Broken Oak, looking closely for a flash of white, a movement that did not belong. Everything remained still, the darkness remained dark, "Too good, Cassias?"

"Maybe there is little here to be drawn back to." His voice grew quiet, as though speaking to himself. "If I could leave this place, I am not sure I would return."

"You think your wife will not come back?" Theodora matched his hushed tone, glancing to ensure Ottoline did not overhear. "What makes you say so, Cassias? Surely, she must come home at some point. One cannot remain at the seaside forever."

"It is quieter without her," he whispered, so softly she almost didn't hear him. His gaze was far away—his mind, it seemed, was too. "So much quieter."

Theodora leaned closer, so close...too close. He was cobweb and sweetness, a strange scent she could not quite place. "What do you mean?"

"I have a secret, Theodora," Cassias said, words tumbling from his lips as though he had not meant them to fall at all. "A terrible one."

He swayed and Theodora caught his elbow, supporting his body with her own as he fell against her, barely upright, head upon her shoulder.

"Papa?" Ottoline looked up with a fistful of grass and weeds. She stared at her father, wide-eyed, before her gaze settled on Theodora.

With a tight smile, and still clutching Cassias, she said, "Ottoline, my love, run up to Ms. Rivers and see if she can wash the mud from your hands, I'll be along in a moment."

"What is wrong with Papa?"

"Now please, Ottoline, before the rain comes in." When the girl hesitated still, she added, "All will be well, likely another migraine and nothing more. Tell Ms. Rivers to put the kettle on, too."

Theodora watched as she ran back up the hill, skirts in hand, disappearing into the shadows of the house. She did not look back. With only the watching crows above for company, Theodora focused on the young lord. "What terrible secret, Cassias?"

She was unsure if she truly wanted to know. Whatever secrets lay hidden within Cassias Thorne were none of her concern. She held her own, heavy and dormant at her breast—she did not think she could bear the weight of another.

"My secret?" he murmured, looking toward the pond where his daughter no longer played. "I can't remember...where is she?"

"Who?"

He staggered back, hand at his head. "Where did she go?"

"Your wife?"

"Where did she go?"

Theodora took his arm. "She is away, Cassias, you know this. Now come, come back into the house with me."

He shook his head but did not protest when she led him away from the pond and back up to the house that seemed to watch them. It kept its silence, that house—kept its secrets as they each kept theirs.

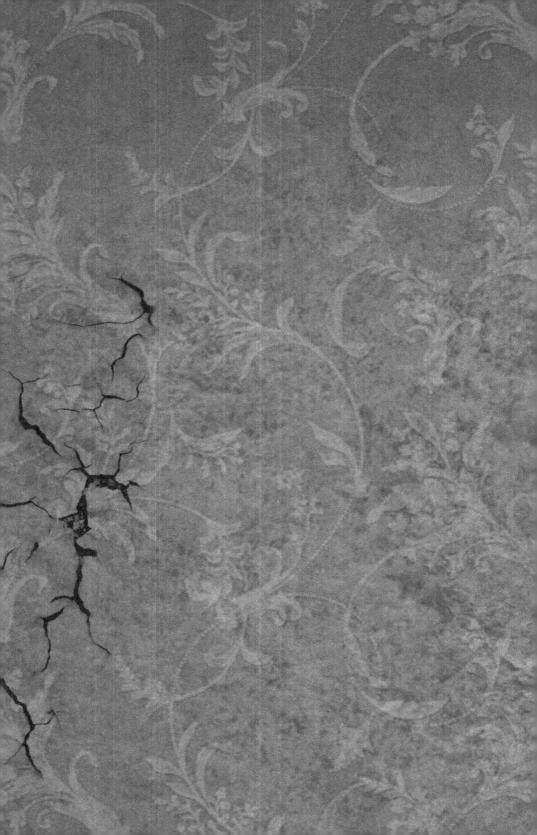

Fifteen

Good people make good places

S he could not sleep, so Theodora took to the halls, restlessly slipping past grand portraits of the lords and ladies who had once stalked those floors. They watched in the darkness, in silence, and all seemed disinterested in her. She found herself in the gallery, the room suspended in moonlight and silence. Theodora stopped before Eleanor's portrait, painted eyes gazing down at her, and they cared. They cared how she trod over the carpets, up and down the stairways, and through the gardens. They cared that she slept beneath her roof and, that once, more than once, she had touched her husband's hand.

Theodora stared back, chin held high, knowing she had done nothing wrong. Nothing to deserve the lady of the house's scorn. She was the daughter of a lord herself, not some lowly servant sniffing at the ankles of her betters. And if perhaps it was a little unusual to find friendship beneath the roof of one's employment, then so be it. Theodora herself was quite unusual.

Following the maze of corridors and hallways, staircases and dead ends, the doubt and worry seeped from Theodora. She enjoyed large houses, the feeling of space, the comforting darkness, the weight of the shadows. She was lost deep in her thoughts when she stepped straight into something solid.

"The devil curse you, Cassias!" Theodora hissed, fighting the instinct to whack the lord again. "What in heaven's name are you doing out at this time of night?" With her hand over heart, Theodora hoped he would not point out that she also was out of bed in the middle of the night.

"This way," he whispered. "It's this way."

Theodora snatched his hand as he made to walk away, allowing herself to be dragged behind him. He stumbled on, one hand trailing over the walls. The other gripped hers tight.

"Cassias—"

"This way."

Theodora wanted to ignore the feel of his fingers around hers—the softness of his palms, the strength of his grip. She wanted to ignore the tightness in her belly, the extra squeeze around her heart as she followed. She could feel his wedding band against her hand, and she wanted to ignore that, too.

"Cassias, please..."

"Come."

He staggered, almost slipping to the floor before Theodora could catch him. She held him around his waist, his body too close to hers. He leant forward, head resting against her shoulder, and went limp.

"Cassias!"

He murmured against her neck, lips brushing her skin in a way no other lips had touched her before. "Follow me."

Theodora had felt the weight of a man against her, felt the clumsy handling of skirts, the staleness of breath both hot and heavy on her skin. She knew what it was to be trapped beneath a body, to go without air or dignity. To wait.

The weight of Cassias against her was different, there was a softness to it, a vulnerability wholly unknown to her. She knew with great certainty that, if she allowed him to fall, then he would fall and not think less of her for doing so.

"You will find yourself quite ridiculous in the morning," she said, giving him a firm nudge. "Never before have I encountered a family of such late-night wanderers."

He lifted his head, eyes unfocused. "This way."

"By your lead, my lord." Theodora rolled her eyes, knowing it would go unnoticed. "Show me what you wish and hurry about it so we can go back to bed."

Cassias Thorne, dressed in no more than his nightshirt, led Theodora through the darkened halls of Broken Oak. She could not help but wonder what her grandmother would say if she knew. For all her talk of adventure, Theodora was certain that she did not intend for her granddaughter to stalk through the darkness with an ill-dressed lord. She made a note not to mention it in her next letter.

The darkness grew solid around them, cold and unwelcoming, as they walked hand in hand up and up and up, past the old servant quarters, to the winding landing that led into the attic. The beams above them creaked—the only part of the house that wished to speak to Theodora. *Come closer,* it seemed to say. *Come see.* It beckoned her, and she could not turn away, could not ignore the whispers of a house that was otherwise silent.

Out in the moon drenched night, the waters of the pond stood still and quiet and, hard as Theodora looked, she could find no sign of any watchers. No one had stayed behind at Broken Oak. No one had waited. She wondered where they had gone, if they were ever there before. Where were those who sought salvation beneath the murmuring eaves of Broken Oak? There was an emptiness to it all, one Theodora felt too keenly.

Cassias staggered ahead, hand heavy in hers. Cobwebs lay thick above them, long abandoned, some still clinging to the dried husks of insects caught in the silk. The whole hallway felt discarded and forgotten—a place Theodora had no wish to be. Ignoring the surrounding gloom, Cassias reached for the brass doorknob shining bright against the grime.

"Stop!"

He startled at her cry, hand halting a breath from the handle. "What—"

"I don't want to know," she said, pulling him back roughly. "Whatever secret you have in there, I do not wish to know, Cassias Thorne!"

"I can hear her," he pleaded, body swaying and eyes empty. "But I can't find her."

His fingers lingered above the handle, those empty eyes dark and wide as they fixed upon hers. Waiting. He waited for her. She gave a quick nod and his hand fell to the brass and turned.

The door held fast, locked and firm. The beams overhead creaked, the floorboards creaked, and the door made no sound at all.

Cassias slipped to his knees, the keening noise at his lips joining the groaning of the house.

Theodora knelt beside him, hands searching for his. "Look at me."

He glanced up, pale and lost against the dirt and grime of the hallway, but she knew that he could not yet see her. Not really.

"Let's go back." She tugged at him and he rose, swaying where he stood. "You can lean against me, Cassias. Come away from here."

The lord of Broken Oak Manor leant heavily against Theodora on the way back to his room, bare feet soundless on the floorboards. He stopped, barely lucid, pulling Theodora to the bedroom just down the corridor from his.

"Ottoline is sleeping, Cassias," she whispered, one firm hand against his shoulder. "Leave her to rest."

"You found her?" The words were delicate and low, his head bent low, eyes to the floor.

Theodora guided his head up with a gentle hand, catching his gaze and keeping it. "She was never lost; she has always been here, with you and with me."

Cassias allowed her to lead him away, to the warm darkness of his room. The candle at his bedside burned low, the fireplace only embers. Theodora noticed the rumpled blankets, the dip in the mattress where he had slept, and looked away.

"Theodora?" Her name was a whisper in the shadows, all soft edges. She turned back to him, seeing his eyes fixed on their tightly entwined hands.

She smiled. "There you are."

He squeezed her hand and said nothing.

"You were sleepwalking again," she said gently. "I wanted to make sure you found your bed safely."

"I think," he began, voice thick. "I had a terrible dream...I don't remember it now, but it was there. I can still feel the stain of it—an inkblot on my mind."

"You were acting strange earlier today," Theodora said, noting how he still clung to her hand. She allowed it, not having the heart to pull away. "Ms. Rivers told me you suffer with headaches, like migraines? Is it like this?"

He nodded, shoulders hunched as though withdrawing into himself. "I apologize once again for having you return me to my bed."

She nudged his arm, wanting to bring him back, to ease the haunted look from his face, the shadows in his eyes. "I thought it would just be Ottoline sneaking out of bed. It is fortunate that Ms. Rivers keeps herself to her rooms or else I would never get any sleep."

His lips moved in memory of a smile. "I would like to promise it will not happen again."

"When it does," she whispered, her hand still locked with his, the softness of him brushing against the softness of her, "I will be here to ensure you do not get lost."

Cassias raked his free hand through his hair, fingers tangling in his curls. "I'm so tired, Theodora."

She gestured to the armchair in the corner of the room, knowing before she uttered the words that she should stop. Be quiet. Be gone. "Would you like me to stay, to ensure you don't wander off again?"

"I couldn't ask you to do that," he replied, voice so very quiet. There was no shock behind them, no outrage at the boldness of her offer, at the impertinence.

"You didn't ask, Cassias."

He waved to the corner of the room, gesturing to a well-worn armchair overloaded with velvet cushions. "Take the bed then, I'll have the chair."

Theodora settled into the plump armchair, shoving a few over-stuffed cushions to the floor. She curled her feet up, her head resting back. "Sleep, Cassias."

He hesitated before climbing under the covers with a sigh. He pulled them high, curling his body tight beneath their weight. Theodora watched as he tossed and turned, blankets knotting around his legs, until at last he stilled and calmed and slept. She watched him from the darkened corner of the room, comfortable and warm, knowing that perhaps she should not have stayed, not have watched. Yet, in that contented darkness, she did stay, the weight around her heart seeming to settle, and she found it easier to breathe.

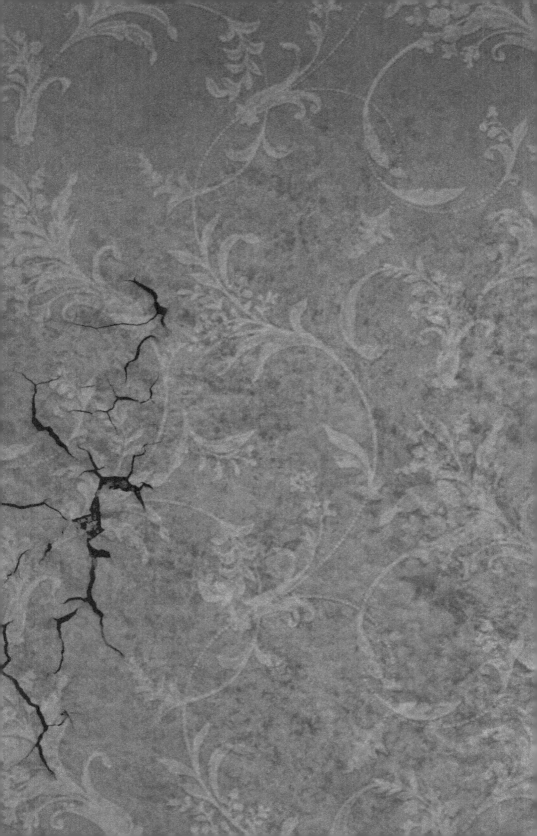

Sixteen

The beginning and end of everything

Theodora left before sunrise, the sky still dark. From her place upon the armchair, she could see the night, the stars that lay scattered in an expanse of black, blinking and watching from so very far away. Moonlight, ashen and cold, poured through the gap in the curtains to spill across the floor. Nothing moved, the shadows remained still, the room uttering not a sound.

Cassias slept on, curled beneath the blankets, dark hair spilled over the pillows like ink. She lingered a moment—to ensure he would not rise again that night, she told herself. It was a convincing lie, one she held onto, clung to, for it was safe and good and pure.

With quiet footsteps, she slipped from the room and down to the kitchen.

"I thought better of you, Miss Corvus," the housekeeper said from the shadows, tea before her on the table, the familiar square of crochet in her hands.

Theodora settled herself opposite, breathing in the scent of bergamot that rose from the teacup. "I do not know what you mean."

"Did you spend the night in your room?" The tone was clipped and harsh.

"I spent half the night following his lordship around the dark corridors of this house, Ms. Rivers," Theodora snapped. "I thought it best that I stay to ensure he did not hurt himself."

The housekeeper's thin, gray brows rose. "He was out of bed?"

"Indeed, he was," Theodora replied, unable to keep the sharpness from her own voice. "Confused and lost; he looked most unwell." She sat back with her arms folded. "Should I have left him?"

The housekeeper remained silent for a moment, slipping wool around her crochet hook. "Where did he wander?"

"To the top of the house; I think he misses his wife."

Ms. Rivers shook her head. "He knows where she is."

"Perhaps, but at night, in sleep, is it that unlikely that he would search for her?"

"Do you think he is, Miss Corvus?"

Theodora caught and kept the housekeeper's gaze, voice lifting. "That he would search for his wife or that he misses her?"

"Does Cassias Thorne miss his wife?" Ms. Rivers's mouth was a thin line, eyes bright and keen.

"I think—"

"What do you think, Miss Corvus?" the housekeeper demanded, though her tone seemed to soften just slightly, sounding weary. "Truly?"

Theodora thought that no one lamented the absence of Lady Thorne. She had yet to hear a kind word about Eleanor Thorne from Cassias—from anyone, for that matter. It did feel that not a soul in Broken Oak suffered from her absence.

Theodora voiced no such thoughts to Ms. Rivers, instead leaning forwards, elbows brushing over the table top. "Do you miss her?"

"I have no reason to," came the reply, with a curl of the lip. Not a smile, there was no humor on the housekeeper's lips.

"Cassias wanted to go to Ottoline last night, and the time before."

Ms. Rivers sat upright, words sharp. "He was looking for Ottoline?"

"She sleeps down the hall from him," Theodora said, noting the housekeeper's look, one she could not place; was it sadness, or something else?

Ms. Rivers set her crochet aside. "If you find him wandering at night again, lead him away from the attic. There is nothing for him there."

"Ottoline is often out of bed too," Theodora said.

The sharpness of the housekeeper's gaze darkened, the candle-light seeming to cling to the edges of her face, leaving the rest in shadow. "Are you quite certain it was her?"

"Who else would it be, Miss Rivers?"

The housekeeper sighed, spooning three sugars into her tea. "Stay away from the attic, Miss Corvus."

The rain cleared by mid-afternoon, leaving a low mist that settled over the grass and lingered by the water's edge. The air itself was damp, heavy, and clung to Theodora's skirts, weighing them down until it became hard to believe that she was ever dry, ever quite warm enough.

Ottoline raced ahead, feet soundless on the gravel pathways that led to the rose garden. She was fey-like in her movements—quick, delicate, and innocent. The sound of her laughter pierced the gloom, shattering it as easily as glass.

She held a sketch book and charcoals; Theodora had set the task of her choosing one of the slumbering roses to capture on paper. To draw the creeping vines and new buds, the dried seed heads that had scattered. She wanted them, black on white, a promise of spring.

"Are you quite sure you wish for me to join you?" Cassias asked, walking beside her, close enough that she could feel the brush of his sleeve against hers.

"It is your house; she is your daughter." Theodora laughed softly. "You do not need an invitation, Cassias."

"I was told that it was not my place to parent her," he said, quiet enough that Theodora had to bend to hear. "That I should be content to know she was being raised as a daughter of a lord should be raised—away from me."

The sounds of Ottoline's laughter disappeared behind the high walls of the rose garden, delighted shrieks echoing around her. Cassias paused, eyes closed as if drawing that sound deep within him, lest he forget it.

"You wanted to school Ottoline yourself?" Theodora asked, placing a comforting hand on his shoulder.

He kept his gaze ahead. "Eleanor deemed it unbecoming and took over her studies. I saw her less and less, and then she would be paraded before me dressed in silks and ribbons for me to compliment before she was taken away again."

"You missed her."

Cassias nodded. "Terribly."

Theodora thought of her own father, how he had kept her at his side, showing her everything the world could be—everything she could be, if only she wished it. Her grandmother had sniffed, tutted, and grumbled at the wildling she was becoming, and her father had laughed and taken Theodora in his arms with no intention of taming her.

He would not have wanted her to become a governess, but Theodora believed that he would not have objected to her being at Broken Oak, taking a young girl under her wing, and allowing her the wildness of all little girls. He would have approved of that; she had no doubt.

"With your wife away, you could be present more in Ottoline's life," Theodora said, hand still on his shoulder.

Before she could think of taking it back, Cassias folded his over it. "And put you out of a job?"

Theodora laughed. "Oh, I believe you will still have use for me, Cassias. One of us will need to discipline Ottoline at times, and I fear it will never be you."

He took her hand, his palms smooth and warm against hers. Their fingers entwined, a gentle pairing, and Theodora knew she ought to let go. It would be best to let go.

"You are a true friend, Theodora," Cassias said, "I am ever thankful you are here, for Ottoline and for myself."

"Then I am thankful that I came here." She did not let go of his hand. "I am thankful for you."

They remained joined as they walked on, steps slow and silent. It was a light touch of hands, a brush of fingertips, yet it stirred something within Theodora's chest, added to the weight of her heart. She wondered whether he felt it too—the echo between them.

"Tell me a happy memory at Broken Oak," she said into the gentle quiet.

Cassias tightened his hand around hers, drawing it closer. He smiled down at her, all softness. "Just the one?"

"One for now."

"Then I shall speak of my earliest happy memory, Theodora," he said, a smile lifting his words. "Before my mother grew ill, and while my father was away, she had the servants push all the furniture in the sitting room against the walls, so that there was one large empty space before us." He stopped walking, turning ever so slightly so that they faced each other, though he gazed toward the shadow of Broken Oak. "She pulled the bedsheets from the beds and had the maids find old ladders and wooden sticks from the garden, so she could construct a tent of sorts...yet it was huge, Theodora, this patchwork creation. We stayed there until after dark, the tent lit up with candles she placed in these holders that spun and spun and made the most beautiful shadows on the fabric walls."

He paused, seemingly lost within that memory. Theodora granted him the moment, knowing well the melancholy that remembering brought. Even the happy memories. Especially those.

"I remember we had hot cocoa," Cassias continued, voice low. "That it was bitter, despite the generous heaps of sugar. I remember falling asleep on the rug, surrounded by cushions and cake crumbs and that I woke up in my own bed once it was morning with no memory of how I traveled there. Like magic."

"Perhaps one evening, you could do the same for Ottoline?" she said, drawing him back. "Ms. Rivers would have a fit."

He laughed, the sound sudden and joyful. "You are a devil, Theodora."

"Thank you for sharing that memory, Cassias," she replied, joining in with his laughter, the sound interlocking the way their hands were. "I am glad that Broken Oak has known joy. I feel a house can absorb the feelings around it."

"There are a few good memories here, Theodora. Some from the distant past, of growing up under its roof," Cassias replied, voice still rich and warm. "Many from the first few years with Ottoline. I feel there will be more good memories in the future. I have hope in them."

Theodora's reply was lost in Ottoline's sudden cry. "Papa, look!"

They slipped apart without a sound, hands still close but no longer touching. Theodora could feel the echo of his warmth as clearly as the absence of it.

"Papa! A crocus, it hasn't bloomed yet, but I found it." Ottoline stopped before them, dirt-covered hand outstretched to reveal the thin, green stalk of an early crocus. "Can we put it in a jar, Miss Corvus, and wait for it to flower?"

Theodora took the plant from Ottoline, dusting the grains of dirt from its broken stem. The roots lay crooked against her palm, hanging from threads.

"Will it flower, Miss Corvus?" Ottoline asked, eyes bright.

Theodora thought of the ill-fated crow from her childhood, how she had plucked it from the earth hoping it would fly again. She smiled down at Ottoline, the lie pressing heavy upon her lips. "I believe with some tender care, it shall."

It would not be difficult, Theodora thought, to creep into the darkness and scoop another bulb from the garden to plant in a jar at the kitchen window and watch it bloom.

Beneath the fine rain and low clouds, they wandered to the slumbering roses, the thin vines clutching the trellis, determined to wait out winter and see spring.

"It has grown wilder with its neglect," Cassias said, trailing a hand over the knotted stalks. "It ought to be hacked back, but I am loath to tame it."

Theodora stood beside him, fingers following the vines up over the trellis, getting thinner as they grew.

"Chop it back and it will grow stronger," she said, hand lingering on a blackened branch. "This disease will spread if not cut out. Cut it down, and it will regrow."

He turned to her, the soft shadows of the winter light gentle on his face. It touched his cheekbones, the dip of his lips, the honey in his eyes. "Stronger?"

Once again, they were too close. "And wilder."

"Should I allow my house to be overrun with wild things, Theodora?" The words ghosted over her cheek, sharp and lovely all at once.

"It is your house, Cassias."

"And I am asking you."

The sound of Ottoline playing nearby faded, the echo of her laughter swallowed by the whispers of Cassias Thorne. He waited for her, too close and yet not close enough. She thought of the sprawling house at the top of the hill, its quiet secrets, the painted frown of Eleanor Thorne, the footsteps in the night.

"Let the roses grow as they are, leave them to grow thin and spindly, they will bloom still."

"But not at their best."

Theodora stepped back, forcing a distance between them. "Perhaps not at their best, but content."

He caught her arm as she turned away. "Are you content, Theodora?"

The weight in her chest tightened. She wanted to pull away, to steer the conversation back to the sleeping roses—knowing too well that they had not been discussing flowers, not truly. She was content. Contentment was fine, expected; a privilege she once thought would not be owed to her again.

"I ask for little else in this life, Cassias."

"Then you ought to." His hand tightened on her arm. "If you are to be wild, then be so and live up to it. Why be less? Why wish for less?"

"I am not lesser for my contentment, Cassias!"

"I meant no offense." His fingers remained where they were. "You have more to give this world, Theodora, I am certain of it. If only you—"

She snatched her arm back, fingers curling with the desire to strike him. "Please do not lecture me on my wants and wishes, Cassias. If I say I am content, then allow me to be content. If I am to be your friend, then let this friendship—"

"Is this friendship?" The words rushed past his lips, harsh and quiet. "Truly, Theodora? I can feel the echo of your hand upon mine, the warmth of your voice in my very soul, and I look for you in each shadowed corner of that damned house. Is that friendship? My wife—"

"Your wife, Cassias!" Her hand landed on his chest, fingers splayed. "You are married. Pray tell, what could you possibly offer me except ruin?"

His hand closed over hers. "My heart. My soul, if you would have it."

"We do not know each other, Cassias. Not truly." It mattered little to Theodora's heart—to whatever part of her called out to him. They were a few shared words, soft touches in moonlight.

"Yet my soul knows yours, Theodora. I can feel it."

"No, Cassias..."

"Is that not enough?"

"How could it be?" The hopelessness of it washed over Theodora, extinguishing the warmth she carried, had clung to, until all that remained was rain-damp skin and a too-heavy heart. "Where would you put me, Cassias? When at last your wife came home? Who else would take me in?"

"And if she never came home?" Cassias demanded, barring her way as she made to pass. "If she remained away from here, what then?"

"Then it would change nothing. I cannot love you. I will not allow it."

"You say that as though it were a choice, Theodora, but it is not. I know it is not, for I believe what you feel for me is what I feel for you against my will and good reason. I cannot choose not to love you."

"Then choose not to act upon it," she replied, chin high, shoulders back to take the weight of her words so she would not buckle beneath them. She nodded to the far corner of the rose garden, to the silhouette of the young girl playing beneath the iron arches. "Remember this feeling, Cassias, and cherish it as I will. Remember it well for the years to come, for when the years take the childhood from Ottoline. Be content in seeing her fall into a love that barely whispered to you."

"Then promise you will stay." He stepped aside, allowing her to pass if she wished. "I will ask nothing else of you."

"When your wife returns, Cassias, I will go." Theodora said, and it felt as though she were giving a piece of herself away, though she felt no lighter for doing so. "You know that I must."

He nodded, the warm brown of his eyes shining. "Not before, I beg of you."

She smiled then, a broken smile that ached. With care, she placed a hand to his cheek, the barest of touches before she drew back with a sigh, with regret. "You have my word, Cassias Thorne."

Theodora swallowed the heaviness in her throat and forced her lips into a larger smile, one that showed a contentment she did not feel, could not feel, and called to Ottoline. The girl skipped soundlessly over the gravel path. Ottoline held a hand out to her father, hesitant, almost shy, her smile as false as Theodora's. Cassias ignored her outstretched hand, instead bending low to sweep her into his arms.

Ottoline sunk into her father's hold, head buried against his neck, fingers tight on his shoulders. She looked like a limpet clinging to a boat's hull.

"Do not let your wife take her away from you," Theodora said softly, and Cassias held Ottoline ever more tightly. "When the time comes for me to go, fight for her."

"I have a lot of time to make up for."

Theodora brushed a curl from Ottoline's face, fingers sweeping over the single dimple on her cheek. The girl smiled, safe and warm and loved.

"This is a perfect start, Cassias. You need to do a little more, nothing less."

They walked back up to Broken Oak together, the words shared between them lingering and heavy, full of wants and desires with no place to go. Theodora took Ottoline from him and settled her into bed. The candles were already lit, the fireplace heaped and hungry. Nothing shifted in the shadows, the windows closed tight against the wind. Nothing moved and nothing whispered.

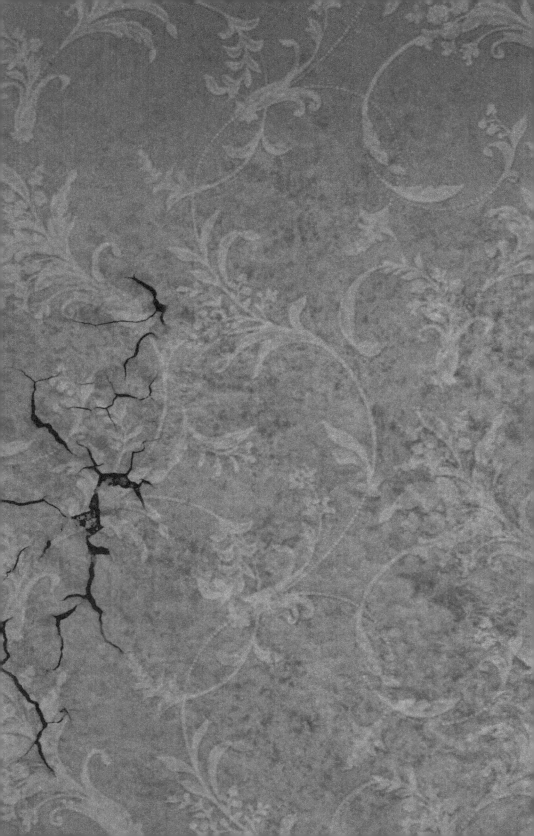

Seventeen

I will sit with you in the dark

S he dreamed of cold waters and black skies, ink-dark and unforgiving. The water pulled her down, down, down, pouring past her mouth to wash the tears down her throat. It was everywhere, breaking the glass to flood through her room's windows, a torrent of ghostly black. It wound its way to the candles, licking at the flame before turning to, and dousing the fireplace. Only darkness remained, thick and final; it tied itself around Theodora, and it would not let her go.

She woke with a cry, feet tangled not in darkness but in blankets. Her bed remained dry, the windows unmarked by dirty water. Although the candle at her bedside had gone out, the fireplace still burned hot. With a trembling hand, Theodora sat up, hand splayed over her bed to cement that she was there and safe and undrowned.

Hearing footsteps, she turned to her door, wondering if her distressed cry had been heard. She called out into the night, voice wavering. "A nightmare, nothing more."

No answer but the footsteps disappearing down the corridor.

"Ms. Rivers?" Theodora called. "Is that you?"

Not wanting to shout again, Theodora rose. Her feet touched the cold wood of the floor, slipping against the mud she had not seen in the darkness. Fumbling for the door handle, Theodora rushed from the room, the name of the housekeeper at her lips. "Ms. Rivers? Are you there?"

Only silence answered her, the echo of footfalls dying away. She wandered down the hall, one hand against the wall, one outstretched to the darkness. The chill of the night wrapped around her, kept close. The shadows lay heavy. Quiet in a way they should not have been. The house spoke not, not a creak or groan. It kept its silence as it kept its secrets, locked away where she could not hear them, find them. It swallowed the sound of footsteps, leaving nothing but her.

She longed for the company of others, away from her lonely room high in the house, with its winding corridors and too-quiet walls. She stumbled, almost weeping in the dark, needing to be down, away, unafraid, and not alone. She wandered past the staring portraits and did not look up, too wary of meeting Lady Thorne's gaze. She rushed past, feet slipping along the floor, soundless and desperate and frightened—on and on until she spotted the flash of white ahead, moving toward her, closer and closer. She stumbled, knees hitting the wood, her cry slipping past the hand she held to her mouth.

"Please..."

"Are you well?" Cassias knelt before her, not quite touching her. "Theodora?"

She wanted to reach out, to find the comfort she knew would be freely given—that it was acceptable to be comforted by a friend when in need, and she was in need. Theodora remained still, and Cassias did not move closer.

"A bad dream," she said, words falling against the palm of her hand. "I am sorry if I startled you."

"I thought you were a ghost." He gave a small laugh, gentle and soft. "We must stop running around these halls at night, Theodora."

She tried to laugh with him, to smile for him. But the ache at her heart was simply too much, too full, too heavy.

"Come," Cassias said, laughter gone. He held her elbow as she stood. "I could walk you back to your room, if you like? As you did for me."

"I do not wish to be alone."

"I could stay, you have a chair in your room?"

She scoffed, warmth settling back into her bones. "It is little more than a stool, Cassias."

"It will do, come on."

He hovered close as they walked along the darkened corridors, back up the unlit staircase to her bedroom. The house was quiet, the shadows unmoving, the trail of mud upon the floor, gone.

"I forget you are up here all alone, Theodora," Cassias said, holding the door open for her. "This floor has always been used for the governesses; for higher ranking staff, as the rooms are larger and well-fitted."

Theodora settled on her bed, feeling foolish when he stood beside her. The room was simply her room, comfortable and plain. "I like this room," she said truthfully. "I am used to sleeping away from others in large houses. It was an unpleasant dream that stirred me tonight, that is all."

"Do you wish for me to go?"

She was no longer fearful, the lingering tremors of the nightmare passing. She did not need him to stay. "You could stay a moment, we could talk."

"About what, Theodora?" Cassias sat on the small chair, legs folding beneath him.

"About anything." She did not want him to go. "Anything at all."

"Why did you leave Kingsward?"

"Anything but that, Cassias," she answered, too quickly, too quietly. "Please."

Cassias said nothing, allowing the silence between them to linger.

It was a gentle silence, one of waiting. In it, he took her hand, fingers folding over hers so very lightly.

"Tell me of your home, Theodora," he said, leaning closer.

She smiled and closed her eyes. "The house is too big and falling to ruin; it will rot around my grandmother and become her tomb, and she cares little. My father did not want it, and he did not want me to want it. Yet it became a part of me, those crumbling walls and fragile timbers. I think, despite myself, I grew to love it." She sighed, remembering Woodrow House as clearly as if she had never left it. "It spoke to me, Cassias, every creak and groan and rattle; it shared its secrets with me, and I never felt alone."

Theodora thought of the specters around the lake, their blank eyes and silent grins watching her from the mist. There were no such watchers around the lilypond at Broken Oak Manor, no one waiting. Why had no one waited?

"You would go back?" Cassias asked, voice low and lovely in the darkness. "To see your grandmother?"

"I hope to." Her hand remained in his, as though it belonged there. She allowed them, for a moment, to belong there. "I sent her letters but have heard nothing in return."

"They were posted?"

Theodora nodded, drawing her legs beneath her. "I gave them to Ms. Rivers, who assured me they would be."

"I could write to your grandmother. Would she reply to the lord of the house?" The teasing tone of his voice did not go unnoticed.

"If you perhaps left the letter vague and hinted at scandal, she would delight in replying."

His laugh was wonderful, deep and real. Again, they found themselves too close, so very close. She had leant toward him and he toward her.

"This is a scandal," Theodora breathed, feeling as though she were falling.

His free hand moved against her shoulder, fingers running through the soft strands of her hair. "Tell me to stop."

She sighed against him. "Don't stop."

"Tell me to go." His lips brushed the edge of her cheek.

"Don't go."

"Tell me..."

Her mouth found his, swallowing the words. He was all soft and slow, pausing to give her room to move away, to stop, to be respectable and end it. The feel of his lips on hers, the warmth of him, they did not feel like scandal or desolation. They felt like home.

Theodora deepened the kiss, hands knotting in his curls, and pulled him closer. His hands found her waist, fingers splayed to draw her to him so not a breath lay between them. Upon the bed they fell, in the gentle darkness with its unmoving shadows. They gathered there, a tangle of arms and legs and heartstrings.

Cassias kissed the hollow of her throat, sending rivers of heat to every nerve, every part of her, until she was aflame. Her name slipped from his lips, a prayer, a litany just for him.

Sweet kisses decorated the pale skin of her neck, her shoulder, down and down to the swell of her breasts. He painted her with his mouth, the brush of his tongue enticing his name from her lips. She was all brightness and heat, lightness and air. Her body knew more than her heart, than her mind, moving subconsciously to his knowing touches.

He held her, reverent. She became unmoored, adrift with the unfamiliarity of it all, pulled under with each drowning kiss.

"I love you, Theodora Corvus," he breathed against her, words a sigh, a whisper, a promise. "I love you."

She found his mouth once more, savoring those words upon her tongue. They were one body, one soul, fitting so perfectly that no space existed between them.

"I should turn you away," she said, unmoving, sinking further, "Save my heart the pain of losing you; I will not bear the weight of it, Cassias, it will smother me."

His teeth grazed over her lip, then drew away. His hands, soft and gentle, framed her face. "I will not part from you, Theodora. I will not send you away. We will go together into the world—away from the darkness of this house, its empty halls. Wherever you go, my love, I will be at your side. I cannot part with you anymore than I could part with my soul."

The promise settled over her like a blanket, warm and safe. "With Ottoline?"

"With Ottoline," he said, thumb caressing her cheek. "To anywhere, Theodora. Anywhere you choose, I will be beside you."

"You'll be ruined." The words were quiet, so few words had the power to wreak such turmoil.

"My ruin would be living without you. I could live with the echo of outrage, of scandal, of dismay. I care little for the thoughts of others, Theodora." His hand brushed over her cheek, though no more tears fell. "I fear I could not live with your absence."

Cassias claimed her mouth and she allowed herself to fall, fully and wholly. If she were to be damned then let it be so, for surely it could be no worse than letting go of him.

They held each other in the darkness, shared kisses and whispers and wonders until their words softened, sleep beckoning. Theodora lay wrapped in his arms, head against the hollow of his neck, their legs entwined. She watched him sleep for a moment, savoring the closeness, the comfort. His lashes cast shadows against his skin, soft lips parted ever so slightly. The fingers locked with hers relaxed and slipped to the mattress and he stilled, lost within the dark folds of slumber.

With a wondrous smile, her heart lighter than it had ever been, Theodora closed her eyes and slept.

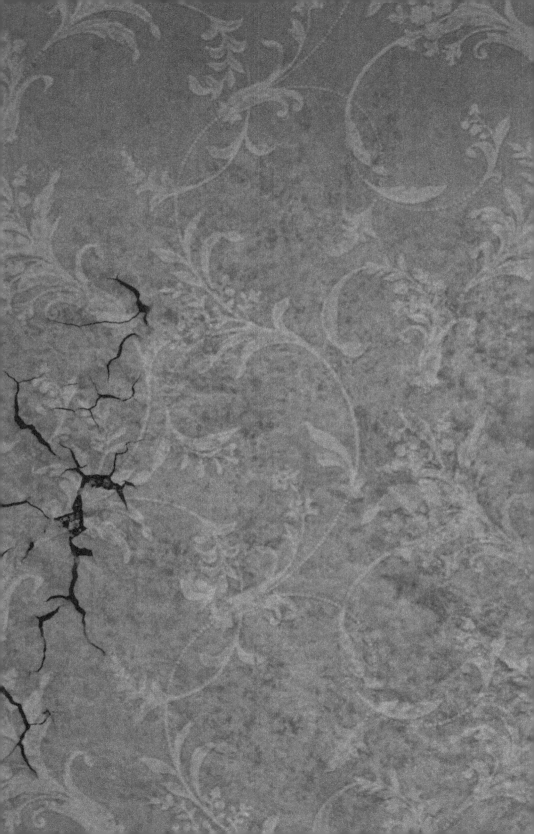

Eighteen

Whatever our souls are made of

⌒

Dearest Grandmother,

I hope this letter finds you and finds you well. I miss the sound of your voice, the feel of your hand. I miss Woodrow House and long to hear news of it. If my letter goes unanswered, I will have to conclude that the walls have finally caved in and there is nothing left but rubble and echoes.

I have much to tell you, too many secrets to spill over ink and paper, so I beg of you, please, write me back; allow me to visit. Allow me to share with you my heart. You once expected more of me, father wished for more. I

have more, Grandmother. The promise of so much more,
yet I fear your judgment. I have need of your blessing.

With love, always.
Theodora

Theodora set her pen aside and waited for the ink to dry before handing the letter to Ms. Rivers.

The housekeeper stood watch at her door, lips a thin line. "I'll have it sent with the next post."

"You are quite certain there have been no letters?"

"I will not have my wits doubted by you, Miss Corvus," came the sharp reply. Her eyes landed just beyond Theodora, to the crumpled bed sheets. "Fitful dreams, girl?"

"I did have a night terror, Ms. Rivers," she answered, refusing to follow the housekeeper's gaze. Cassias had left near dawn, gently untangling himself from her and leaving a lingering kiss upon her cheek.

The lines against Ms. Rivers's mouth softened. "This house likes to bestow its occupants with strange dreams."

"Do you have them?"

The housekeeper paused, looking to the fireplace, to the dying glow of the coals. "Not anymore."

"What would you suggest to keep them at bay?"

"Time," Ms. Rivers replied, voice quiet. "They will go in time, Miss Corvus, when you settle, when the house settles around you."

"Cassias is kept awake with them," Theodora began, wary, unsure if she should speak of such things with her. "Does he need more time? To feel the weight of this house settling around him?"

Ms. Rivers's gaze tipped up, looking beyond her little room, toward the eaves of the house. "Time will catch up with Cassias Thorne, Miss Corvus. Will you stand at his side when at last it does?"

"I don't understand."

"There is nowhere you can go," Ms. Rivers said, not unkindly, "where the secrets of this house will not follow you."

"And what secrets are those?"

Long fingers brushed against Theodora's cheek, work-rough and cold. "Wake up, Miss Corvus."

Theodora flinched away. "Take your hand off me." Her glare met Ms. Rivers's narrowed eyes.

The housekeeper's lips thinned, the lines around them deep and harsh. She retreated, folding the letter into the pocket of her apron. "Your skirts are damp, Miss Corvus, do dry them off before you get a chill."

Theodora watched her slip back into the darkness, the ghost of her hand still cold on her skin. Across the floor, illuminated by the dying light of the fire, were muddied footprints. Shallow puddles of brackish water pooled around her feet, dripped from the window, trickled down the walls to soak into her skirts. She could see no burst pipe, no leaking fixtures, and yet the water dripped. It dripped and it dripped and it dripped.

Rare winter sunlight slipped through the large library window, catching the spines of the old books gathering dust upon the shelves. Overhead, the candles were unlit, the space below cozy and intimate. Theodora reclined on one of the armchairs, skirts drying in the soft warmth. She paid no heed to the strange housekeeper, wondering if perhaps age was creeping up and taking her wits before it took the rest of her. In the soft light of day, it was easier to dismiss the water puddling in her room. The house was old, the windows let in the drafts and could just as easily let in the rain. Perhaps the shadows played tricks on her, dancing in the candlelight to look as though water flowed from the walls.

When Theodora was a child, her father once brought home a delightful new toy, all silver and shining. He had lit a candle and placed it inside and told her to watch as figures waltzed across her walls. The water was just that, she told herself, shadows and light.

Ottoline had been left with a pile of books to read through for the afternoon. She had been tasked with choosing her favorite and reciting a passage from it to the rest of the household later. Ottoline had searched the abundance of books, passing them to Theodora. Some were worn and well read, where others looked as though they had yet to be touched, to be opened. Theodora said nothing regarding the amount of books Ottoline was handing her, simply happy to see her so engaged, so keen to learn,

"Do you have any thoughts on what poem you may choose, Ottoline?" Theodora had asked, watching on as the young girl clambered up the library ladders. "I believe there are some lovely botany books over by the far window."

"I am not searching for sonnets on sunflowers, Miss Corvus," came the reply above her. "I am very much looking for...ah!" She dropped a book down to Theodora with a bright smile. "Romance!"

Theodora tucked the book onto her wavering stack of poetry. "Poems of the heart, a fair choice indeed."

"I think this house needs more romance," Ottoline had said, stepping down from the ladder. "Don't you agree, Miss Corvus?"

Thoughts of Cassias slipped through her mind, the feel of his hand on hers, the softness of his curls, his lips, the words he breathed against her ear. His daughter looked up at her, blue eyes wide and all seeing. There was a smile at her rosebud lips, a childlike cunning.

"My stepmother is not fond of such things," Ottoline continued, her spark fading. "She is fond of little, really. Her heart is a shallow thing, quickly filled and I think it is too filled with papa, and it left no room for me."

"Ottoline—"

"You have room for me, Miss Corvus. I know you do and I know your heart is full and I know it is filled with Papa, but I know I fit there too."

With care, Theodora set the books she carried down, then pulled the girl close, as close to her overfull heart as she could, where the weight of it ached. Ottoline fit there, as did her father, and there was even a small space set aside for Ms. Rivers.

"You fit within my heart quite snuggly, Ottoline, and there I shall keep you."

Ottoline had withdrawn with a smile, though it was still not quite as bright as before. She turned back to the small mountain of books, finally settling on a weathered book of poetry, its faded cover depicting a watercolor rose entwined around the gold-embossed letters of its title. Ottoline had left the library on light feet, determined that her recital would be perfect, and Theodora had watched her go with a fond smile.

Looking out at the sweeping lawns of Broken Oak Manor with its bare trees and mist-covered pond, Theodora could not help but imagine herself back at Woodrow, beneath the groaning weight of her family home, with the sounds of her grandmother's rattle; the memories that lived there and just beyond. She wondered where they would go—Cassias, Ottoline, and herself—where life would take them if they were to leave the silent house with its dark corridors and strange dreams.

Then the thought came unbidden: if the quiet house with its hidden secrets would allow them to leave at all.

She became lost in her thoughts, deep within memories and fragile hope for the future, so did not see the shadow move, stretching over the library floor—until it was upon her. It slipped beside her, long and dark, fingers curling over her shoulders. She startled, near toppling to the floor but for the hand that caught her.

"I will have a bell around your neck, Cassias Thorne! Have no doubts about that!"

"I called your name twice." His hand lingered on her arm, barely a touch. "Where did you go, Theodora Corvus?"

He settled into the opposite armchair, fingers interlocked with hers. They were close, knees nearly touching, yet she wanted more.

"Lost in memory." Her hands trailed over the back of his, over his knuckles, tracing the pale blue lines beneath his skin. She lingered on his wedding band, and he pulled away.

"It will not come loose," he said, twisting the golden ring on his finger. "I fear it may have to be cut off."

"I am sure Ms. Rivers would oblige." Theodora took his hand, bringing it to her lips. She smiled against his fingers. "I am sure she would delight in aiding this torrid affair."

"Torrid?" His laugh swept across her face. "Is that what this is?"

"Torrid, scandalous, one might even call it blasphemous with all that talk of lopping off your wedding ring." She shared his smile, his laughter, quiet and secret and theirs. "What would you call it, then?"

"Surprising," he breathed and gently tugged her to him, so they shared the same space. "Wonderful." He kissed her, long and slow. "Salvation."

"Cassias…"

"You are my salvation, Theodora Corvus." His praise died as his lips met hers, disappearing into the narrow space between them, the void where she sealed away all her doubts, all her worries and misgivings.

She kissed him back, twisting against the weight within her chest, finding a place in it for the bliss she felt, room for him to fit there.

Cassias touched her cheek, feather soft. "Have I upset you?"

She followed his touch, finding the teardrop. "Oh! No, no…"

Theodora tried to swallow the tears, the lump forming against her throat. The weight in her chest ached.

"Theodora?"

The softness of her name upon his tongue undid her, and she fell into his arms with a desperate sob. An apology burst from her lips, thick and anguished, and he listened, arms tightening as if he alone could hold her together.

"Is it something I have said?"

She shook her head, unable to reel back the flood, her heartstrings no longer an anchor.

"Is there anything I can do?"

Another shake of her head. She pressed the heels of her hands against her eyes—yet still she wept, and could not stop.

"You do not need to hide your tears from me, Theodora, there is no shame in them." He held her ever tighter, her head resting against his throat. The scent of coal dust filled her senses, along with something sweeter, a strange familiar scent she could not place. "I care to see them."

She wept against him with all the weight of her unshed tears and he held her, and listened, and did not tell her to stop. There they stayed, entwined and content, their voices whispered and soft. With the sun still clinging tight to the winter afternoon, Theodora dozed in Cassias's embrace, feeling that she could breathe again at last.

That evening, they all gathered in the sitting room, candlelight dancing over the edges of the walls, softening the shadows. The fire crackled in the grate, stoked high to keep the chill at bay. The curtains were drawn against the windows, sealing in the warmth, the light.

A comforting quiet settled over the room. Ms. Rivers worked on her crochet, feet propped on a footstool. Theodora sat beside her, lounging back into plump pillows. Cassias sat in his armchair, a good space away from them. Across that distance, he shared a smile with her—one of knowing they were joined in more than flesh.

Ottoline fussed with her skirts, dusting imagined specks from her shoes before she announced that she was ready for her recital. She beamed at them all, nose crinkling as her father leaned forward to listen.

"What poem have you got for us, Ottoline?" Theodora asked, sitting straighter.

Ms. Rivers set down her crochet.

"I have chosen this one because it is a love story, Miss Corvus, and I have always enjoyed a romance."

Theodora risked a glance toward Cassias, his lips echoing her smile. "Oh really? I cannot wait to hear it."

The young girl shuffled on her feet, clasping jittery hands behind her back, before beginning. Ottoline's words started off quiet and unsure, voice faltering ever so slightly. The others listened, eager-eared to the sound of love and hope and wonder, the words spilling from the book clasped before Ottoline.

They fell, those simple words with a gentle perfection, Ottoline's voice growing bolder with each line. She held her chin high, reciting each line of the poem without error, bright eyes darting from Theodora to her father. It was a simple verse, not overly long or weighed with metaphor or deeper meaning. It held no secrets beneath its simplicity. But it was lovely, chosen with such care by Ottoline, chosen for the romance of it, the gentle sweetness and Theodora thought no lovelier words could have been spoken.

At its end, Theodora glanced at Cassias, hoping to share a smile, a knowing look. She was not prepared for the grim set of his lips, the tight clench of his hand upon the armrest.

The last words faded into the hungry quiet. Silence followed. Ottoline paused, rooting into her pockets to find the small book of poetry. "Did I make a mistake?" she asked, voice small and uncertain.

"Where did you get that book?" Cassias demanded, rising.

"The library, Miss Corvus helped me pick it out."

"Cassias?" Theodora stood, taking the book from Ottoline. She had sensed the shift in his mood, how he drew into himself as though his daughter's words had wounded him. She flicked to the front, to an inscription penned in neat, lovely script.

My dearest, my heart, my Rose,

Allow these words to speak what I am often at a loss to say. Take them to heart and keep them there, keep me there, for you are kept in mine. I am yours eternal, my darling.

With all my heart, for now, for always. Cassias.

"This belonged to your first wife." Theodora turned the pages with delicate fingers, noting the gold edges, the frayed ribbon book-mark. "I didn't know, Cassias...I didn't think to look."

"Please give me the book, Theodora."

She held it out to him, and he snatched it. For a moment, he held it close to his chest, his heart, as though reprinting those words upon his soul.

"Did I do something wrong?" Ottoline asked, words trembling.

"Just go to your room, Ottoline," Cassias replied, fingers digging into the book's spine. "Now! Please." The last word rasped from his throat.

Ms. Rivers took Ottoline's hand as the girl stood pale white and sad before her father. With a few murmured words, the housekeeper led her from the room, into the darkness beyond.

"Cassias—"

"Leave me be, Theodora, I beg of you."

She closed the distance between them, guiding him back into the armchair. She knelt before him, hands cupping his, caging the small book between them.

"You are allowed to grieve, Cassias," she said. "Some losses leave scars upon our hearts; wounds that, no matter the time gone by, still ache, still sting when touched. Sometimes, it does not go away, that pain, but it may lessen until, like now, something scratches it and leaves you raw."

He leaned forward, head resting upon her hands, upon the book, upon the words scribbled to a love long gone. "She took her portrait down."

"Eleanor did?"

He nodded, fingers gripping hers. "She tore it from the wall and shoved it in the attic."

Theodora thought of Lady Thorne's cold eyes, her painted indif-ference. She wondered what the first Lady Thorne would have looked like, whether love and kindness had been blended into the canvas.

"There is no shame in holding on, if you are not ready to let her go."

"And if I am never ready, Theodora? What then?" His words were raw, ragged, as if they physically pained him. "You hold my heart now, yet I still feel the echo of her."

She unlatched one hand and placed it over his heart. "There is room here for those you wish to love, Cassias. Ottoline is here, your first love is here. I am here, as you are in my heart, beside the others I love."

"I looked for her, when she passed," he began, voice far away. "I thought perhaps she would wait for me, but I never found her."

The lake at Woodrow House slipped into her mind, unbidden. The faces of black-eyed specters watching from the mist. They waited and waited, and Theodora did not know who for. Like Cassias, she had sought out the faces of those she had loved and lost, both relieved and dismayed when she could not find them. There were no such watchers around the waters at Broken Oak, no one waiting.

"Who did wait? At the edges of the pond?" Theodora asked. "If anyone at all?"

He said nothing for a moment, gaze turning to the window, to the mist-covered waters beyond the house. "No one."

"Not a soul?"

His eyes flicked to hers, shadowed and stark. "Not for a while. If there were souls before, anything that lingered, they are gone now"

"It is late, Cassias." Theodora stood, hand outstretched, wishing to talk no more of what haunted Broken Oak, and what had waited at the water's edge. "Come, let us go to bed. Put these memories to rest, allow them to weave into our dreams where they belong."

He stood beside her, holding the little book close to his chest. "Join me?"

She blinked. "Join you?"

A small smile lifted the edges of his tired mouth, softening the shadows that still remained there. "As I joined you last night in your bed, Theodora, please join me tonight in mine."

"I..."

"Say one reason you cannot."

"It is your marital bed, Cassias," she replied, as though it truly mattered. They had slumbered beside each other once before—shared a bed, breath, whispers, and more.

"I do not want to be alone with my thoughts."

She had no other excuses and did not try to find more. "I do suppose your bed is much larger and finer than mine."

"It is indeed, Theodora Corvus, so bring your cold feet and damp skirts and let us retire."

"My skirts are well past dry now, Cassias!" She found joy in his smile, the shadows that had swept across his face lightening, releasing him from the grip of memory and sorrow.

"If you say so," he said, allowing himself a final glance at the little book of poetry before setting it down on the table. "But your feet are still unbearably chilly."

"I can take my cold feet elsewhere."

His fingers lingered on the book for a moment before his hand ran along Theodora's arm, locking around her fingers before he spun her. Her skirts twirled out, simple and plain. Cassias saw past that—past the lack of shine to her hair, the mud that constantly darkened her hems, past all the things that did not matter—until he saw all of her. As she saw all of him. And they were beautiful.

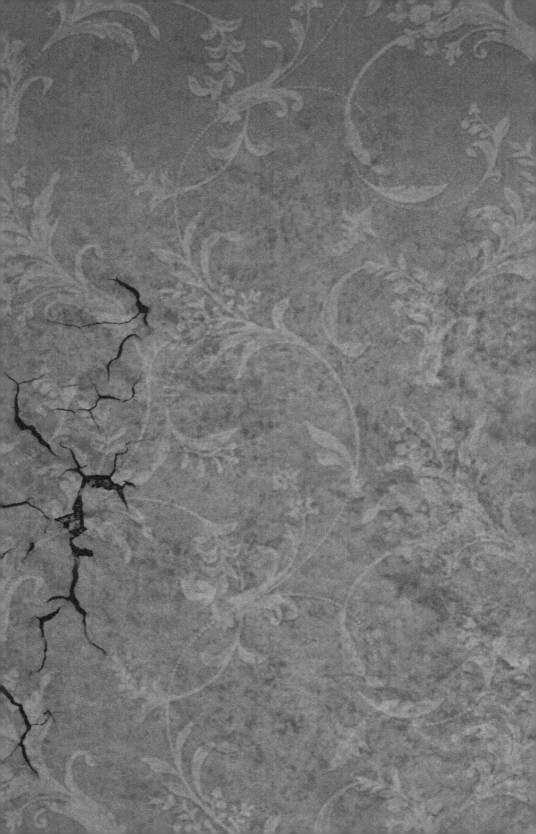

Nineteen

The beginning and end of everything

Cassias led her through the darkened hallways of Broken Oak and up the grand staircase with its twisting banisters to his bedroom. They halted near the door close to his, hearing nothing from the child within. Cassias lingered there, one hand splayed on the door. He stood so still that, for a moment, Theodora wondered whether he was even breathing.

"You can speak to her in the morning," she said, coaxing him away with a gentle touch. "Speak of her mother, Cassias. Ottoline lost someone she dearly loved too. Let her sleep now, let us sleep."

"I would like to give her the book," he whispered, words fragile. "Something touched by both of us."

She leaned into him, hand tight around his. "I think that would be wonderful."

Cassias opened his door for her, leading her toward the large bed dominating the space. The shadows wrapped around the bedposts, drifting along the floor in time with the flames in the fireplace. The intimacy of that waltzing dark slipped over her skin like a caress.

Although she had been in his room before, watched him sleeping, and slept beside him, there was something new about sharing his bed. Something more.

"To sleep, nothing more, Theodora," Cassias said, answering the question on her face. "Just be beside me, please."

She sat upon the bed, feeling the softness beneath her, the expensive sheets, the goose-down pillows. Her hand brushed over the space, the bed almost the size of her room. She gazed up at him. "Nothing more?"

The deep brown of his eyes seemed to darken, turning the color of burnt sugar. "What else would you like, Theodora?"

The pillows were exquisite against her back. Her skin felt not quite her own. She wanted his mouth to be on hers again, his hands to tangle in her hair. She longed for the low moans he uttered when she touched him in return. She wanted that, and she wanted more.

"All of you."

Cassias moved silently with dreadful slowness to the bed. Carefully, he climbed across Theodora, caging her body with his own. He claimed her lips, fingers working at the fixtures of her gown. They became a rush of hands, of hungry mouths and desperate sighs. He pulled off his shirt and yanked the stubborn frock from her bones, tossing them aside until they were stripped bare.

"Stay with me." The words fell upon her with a sigh. "Do not journey back to that lonely little room, Theodora. Stay with me."

"For tonight?"

"For always," he breathed, "until we leave this place, leave Broken Oak far behind us, then be at my side each night after, wherever it is we go."

He lowered himself onto her, lips on hers, hands at her softness, gentle. Patient. They came together with a shared breath, a sigh, a gasp. The world ended and began with them, scorching and consuming until there was nothing left but to fall. And fall they did, bodies nothing, souls colliding, an explosion of stardust.

Cassias held her after, as though she were a precious thing. She lay her head against his chest, his heart quiet, body still save the fingers that ran up and down her arm. She peered up, smiling, and he met her mouth with a slow, full kiss.

In his arms, clothed once more, she fell asleep, lulled into dreams by his closeness. The weight at her chest had shifted, the flood of her tears making room for him, for Ottoline. It ached still, but it was a good ache, one she cherished, one she no longer had to curve her body around.

~

The crash of broken glass hauled Theodora from a sleep so deep, so dark, it took a moment for her senses to catch up. She fumbled for Cassias's arm, feeling the solid weight of him beside her.

"Did you hear that?" she whispered into the darkness.

Cassias stirred, one arm still tight around her body, and mumbled, "Hear what?"

They listened to the quiet, the pause tense and bated. Then a wail that rattled the walls.

Cassias shot up, gripping Theodora's arm. "What the devil was that?"

"You heard it too?"

"Someone is in the house."

The wail rose from beneath them, mournful and broken. Angry. Louder it screamed, louder and louder, a cacophony of fury and madness. The chorus of rage reached a crescendo, trailing off before it was joined by the screech of splintered glass.

"Stay here!" Cassias bolted from the bed. A frightened cry left his mouth as the door flew open, and he staggered backwards.

"Papa!" Ottoline ran into the room, straight into her father's arms. Cassias drew her close and tight as she buried her head in his shoulder and cried, "In my room! It was in my room!"

Theodora slipped from the bed to stand beside Cassias, one hand on the child trembling in his arms.

"Take Ottoline," he said, looking out into the darkened corridor. "I will see what is causing such a ruckus."

Ottoline held on tighter. "No, Papa!"

"I will go see." Theodora stepped into the shadows. "I would like to know why this house is so set against me getting a full night's sleep."

"You cannot go alone, Theodora."

She felt his hand close over hers, fitting around hers so perfectly, as though meant to be there. "Then come with me, Cassias Thorne."

Cassias pressed a kiss to Ottoline's forehead, shifting so she rested against his hip. "You are safe, my darling. I will not allow you to come to harm."

Ottoline gazed back, eyes wide and frightened. "Do you promise?"

"You have my word."

The barest of whimpers fell from Ottoline's mouth before she buried her head against Cassias's shoulder.

Together, they went into the dark, down the unlit corridor, to Ottoline's bedroom. All was quiet and still. All as it should be. The candle beside her bed gave off a welcoming glow, the fireplace burned low, banishing shadows and darkness to the far corners.

From Cassias's arms, Ottoline pointed at the rocking chair—at the cracked plaster behind the headrest where the chair had struck with such force that the wood had fractured.

"I saw someone here," she whispered, "I saw her white skirts."

Cassias gently passed Ottoline to Theodora and ventured out into the hallway, not looking back toward the rocking chair. The unloved doll, Theodora noticed, was sitting on the chair's cushions, its painted eyes staring up at them.

"I asked you to put Juliet away, Miss Corvus," Ottoline whispered in her ear.

Theodora kept her gaze on the doll. "I did."

Theodora followed Cassias, not wanting to remain in the

bedroom a moment longer, knowing it went against all reason to be fearful, yet fearful she was.

They went on in silent footsteps, down into the quiet house with its quiet secrets. There were no echoes of screams or crashes of broken glass.

With careful steps, they entered the shadowed foyer. The candles that remained lit during the night—every night without fail—were out. Only the fire burned, casting a soft glow that caressed the glass shards littering the floor.

"What in heaven's name—"

They all startled at the voice, Ottoline's distressed cry ringing in Theodora's ear.

"This household has quite the habit of sneaking up on unsuspecting folk," Theodora snapped, fear and shock making the words harsh. "We were all awoken by the noise, Ms. Rivers."

"As was I," the housekeeper said, looking between Theodora and Cassias. She shook her head, the movement so slight it could have been mistaken for a trick of the light. Her eyes though, held not contempt, but a strange sadness. "Perhaps it was a stray cat."

"A cat?" Cassias choked out a laugh. "We heard the most awful screams, Ms. Rivers."

"Two cats perhaps." She moved closer to the mess on the floor, bending to pick up a shard. "Only a vase, one of the window panes, nothing more. It echoed in this large space, that is all."

"We had barn cats at Woodrow House, Ms. Rivers," Theodora began, shifting Ottoline in her arms. "I can assure you I know what it sounds like when they all get together."

"Then what do you suppose it was, Miss Corvus?"

She bristled at the housekeeper's tone, the curl of her thin lips. "Could it have been a thief?"

"It could have been the wind." Ms. Rivers plucked another shard from the floor, holding the two pieces close as if, by will alone, she could put them back together. "It could have been anything, Miss Corvus, I can only speculate."

Theodora turned her back to the housekeeper, leaving her to collect the shattered remains of what had actually been quite a hideous vase. "What do you think, Cassias?"

He did not answer, instead wandering away from her, deeper into the shadows of Broken Oak. Theodora carefully set Ottoline down beside Ms. Rivers, following Cassias out of the foyer and into the gallery. She met the cold painted stare of Lady Thorne, feeling as though the woman could see right into her and find her sins. She spun at a low gasp from Cassias, followed by her own cry.

His portrait—that beautiful, gentle likeness of him—bore crude tears down its middle, the strikes so violent they had hewn the wall behind. It had been struck and struck again—blade ripping the canvas over and over as though one sharp blow would never have been enough. There was a brutality to it, so much anger and hate that Theodora could not bear to look.

Cassias staggered away from the ruined canvas, hand at his mouth. She caught his elbow, taking his weight.

"Could it be your wife?" she asked, daring another glance to the slash at his painted neck, the slices down his cheeks. "Would she do this?"

"I...no...she couldn't..."

"Because she is away?" Theodora gave him a firm shake. "Cassias?"

"Away..."

She shook him harder. "Where is your wife, Cassias?"

"I don't... I don't know." He pressed a hand to his head, words slurring. "Theodora..."

She managed to catch him as he fell, knees buckling under the weight, so she crumpled to the floor beside him. His head lolled against her, body limp and useless.

"Ms. Rivers!"

The housekeeper appeared a breath after her voice's echo died, eyes widening at the lord of the house lying on Theodora's skirts.

"He saw the painting...and fainted."

"Papa?" Ottoline rushed to her father, dress spilling out around her as she knelt beside him, small hands brushing the curls from his face.

"Shock, my little darling," Theodora said, taking the girl's free hand. "Sometimes, when someone gets a fright, it is too much and they fall; it's not for long, and it will not hurt him."

"Then why did you cry out, Miss Corvus?"

She squeezed Ottoline's hand. "Because it startled me."

"You did not faint."

Theodora gave her a small smile. "No, I did not."

Ms. Rivers stood close, eyes narrowed and lips pursed, though she said not a word to Theodora. It was an unreadable expression; Theodora thought it not quite pity, not contempt—perhaps weariness. The housekeeper looked tired, as though her bones, like the bones of grand houses, were simply too old.

"Morning is not too far away; how do you feel about spending the small hours with me, Ottoline?" Ms. Rivers asked, eyes and tongue softening. She held out a hand, pulling Ottoline to her side. "The fire is lit in the sitting room, my dear. We can curl up near it and tell stories."

"I wish to stay with Papa." Ottoline remained rooted, eyes never straying from her father.

"Having you hover over him will not help, child. Come with me." Ms. Rivers began to guide Ottoline away, tone firm, hands kind. The girl turned to Theodora as though she would protest, to have her stay.

"Go rest a moment, dear Ottoline," Theodora said. "All will be well, I promise you."

Ottoline's gaze fell upon her father, before rising again to meet Theodora's. "If you say so, Miss Corvus."

The housekeeper gave Theodora a small nod, a silent question in her gray eyes. Theodora gently patted Cassias's cheek, and he stirred.

"I will look after him, Ms. Rivers."

"I hope you will, Miss Corvus," she replied, leading Ottoline away.

"Cassias?" She tapped him again, watching his eyelids flutter. "Can you hear me? Don't sit up yet."

He mumbled something, words thick and strange.

She leant closer. "What did you say?"

"Attic..." The word tumbled from his lips before his eyes rolled back.

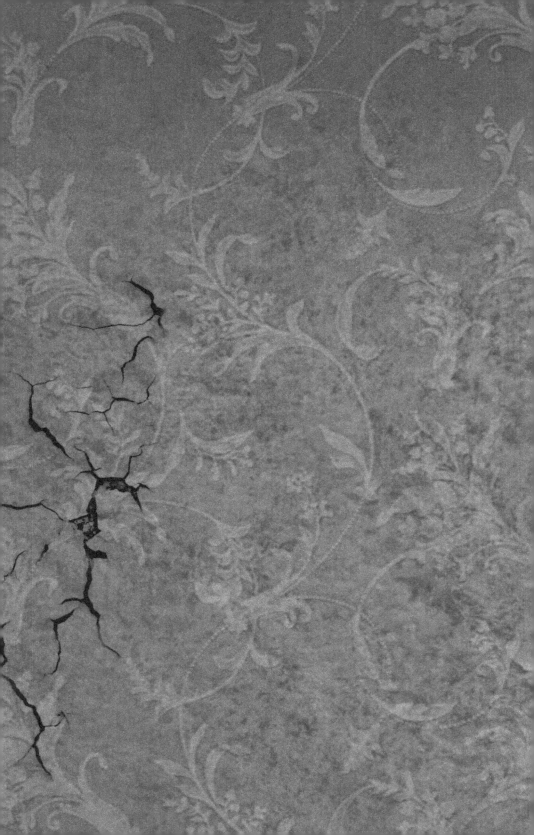

Twenty

Suspicion always haunts

With some effort, and many whispered curses, Theodora managed to get Cassias to his feet. He leaned against her, heavy, wavering with every step along the corridor to his room. The shadows shifted around them, the candlelight wavering as though it, like the rest of them, was disturbed by the night's events. There was movement where there should have been none. She helped him over the threshold of his bedroom, across the soft rugs to the overly large bed.

"Ottoline..." Cassias mumbled, twisting against her hold. "Where..."

"She is with Ms. Rivers." She struggled to get him moving again, her patience slipping. "You are to lie down, Cassias, do you understand me?"

He blinked at her. "Do not raise your voice to me."

She withdrew her hold, allowing him to slip to the floor in an undignified heap. "Can you find your feet on your own, Cassias

Thorne? No? Then I dare say I can speak to you in whatever tone I see fit."

With staggered, clumsy movements, Cassias forced himself upright, hands braced against the wall. He looked at her waiting hand, saying nothing as he reached for it.

Theodora guided Cassias to the bed, keeping her hand locked in his. "How are you feeling?"

He lay back against the pillows, quiet and weary. "Better, thank you," he replied, voice fragile.

She took in his shadowed eyes, the shaking hand he held to his head. "You do not look it."

"This is not how I wanted to end this night, Theodora."

She squeezed his hand. "It has yet to end, Cassias. I will not leave you. I will remain at your side, if you will have me here."

"You have minded me, as much as Ottoline, it seems," Cassias said softly.

"You are not a bother to me."

A tired smile tugged at his lips. "I feel that is a little untrue, Theodora."

"Perhaps a little bothersome then." She placed a small kiss on his brow, brushing aside his dark curls. "I would do it for no other man,"

He sighed, sounding so very tired. "Then I am honored, Theodora."

"Who do you assume ruined your portrait?" she asked, guiding the conversion back to the gallery, the torn canvas, the violence of it all.

His eyes met hers, nearby candlelight picking out the golden flecks within the deep brown. "I think..." He trailed off, sinking back into the soft pillows, eyes closing.

Theodora shook his shoulder, not wanting to be left alone in the dark. "Cassias, please."

"Can it not wait until morning? My head will be clearer then."

"We need to speak of this tonight, what if whoever did this is still in this house?" She could feel her voice rise, feel the frustration grow in her throat, hardening her words.

"Let me sleep, Theodora," Cassias murmured, turning away from her. She could sense sleep settling over him, soft and deep. Her thoughts were a whirlwind, unsettled and disturbed. No peace would find her; she knew that.

"Stay awake," she demanded, poking the young lord sharply in the chest.

He swatted her hand away, eyes still closed. "You told me to rest. I am resting, you contrary woman."

"You can rest without sleeping; we need to talk about this, about you."

He mumbled something she could not quite make out, the words lost as he buried himself deeper in the pillows.

"There are secrets within this house, Cassias Thorne, secrets within you." She shook him again, fingers digging into his arms. "And you will tell me."

He sat upright, pulling out of her grip. "I do not know what you are speaking of."

"What is in the attic?" she demanded. A chill slipped around her, settling across her shoulders like a cloak. "Where is your wife, Cassias?"

"At the coast," he bit back, sitting straighter.

Theodora gripped his hand, caging it with both of hers. "Then who slashed the painting?"

"I do not know!" His voice rose, sleepiness fading from his eyes. They became black pits, hard with a sudden fury. "Perhaps it was Lady Thorne! Perhaps she stole away into the night to wreak havoc upon the family heirlooms." He wrenched his hand away and smiled at her, all teeth. "Or perhaps you think me the reason she does not return, Theodora Corvus, that she has fallen foul of me, and I have stashed her away in the attic—"

His head whipped to the side as she struck him hard. "What an awful thing to say!"

"Did you truly think no such thing?" he asked, hand on his cheek. "Can you, with any honesty, say the thought did not cross your mind?"

Theodora looked up to the ceiling, up past the floorboards, to the rooms above, to the long corridor at the very top of the house— the only space in the sprawling maze that whispered to her.

Her gaze found his, the wonderful gentleness in his eyes hardened and cold. "I would not give my heart up to someone I thought capable of such a thing."

"You do not think me capable, or you wish to believe I am not?" he said, toneless.

"There is little difference. Cassias."

"I think there is," he stated, drawing away from her, forcing a distance that, in truth, had never really been there. From the beginning, they had been drawn to one another, seeking a touch, a kind word—always more than friendship.

She reached for him across the expanse of space, the breath between them. "Then tell me what is in the attic."

He sighed, gaze lingering on her before he looked to the locked room far above. "I...I don't..."

"If you will not tell me, Lord Thorne, I will find out myself." She threw the words at him, and he recoiled. She did not wait—not for excuses, not for reasons, not for whispered half-truths. Without looking back, Theodora slipped into the darkness beyond the bedroom door.

She heard him follow, the sound of her name frantic on his lips. Up she went, past the old servant quarters, up again and again to the narrow winding hallway nestled in the eaves. The house creaked around her, its bones shifting with each of her footsteps, too eager to spill the secrets the lord of the house would not.

"Please come away, Theodora," Cassias pleaded. He tried to take her hand, but she wrenched it free. "There is nothing up here."

"I don't believe you." Another step, a groan of wood beneath her. *Keep going*, it whispered, *come see.*

"Let us go back." He snatched at her hand, locking her fingers between his. "I don't want to be up here, Theodora."

"Then you go back," she hissed. "I am weary of secrets."

"I am begging you..."

"Remove your hand from me, Cassias!" She reached for the door handle, fingers wrapping around the cold brass still shining against the dirt and age of its surroundings. The door would not give, would not yield. The wood sighed against the frame, the house held its breath. All was silent and unmoving.

"Please come away!" Cassias made to grasp the hand on the brass, fingers hard and rough, desperate. Frightened. Theodora lurched back as though burned, and Cassias's hand fell upon the door handle. With the softest of clicks, it swung open.

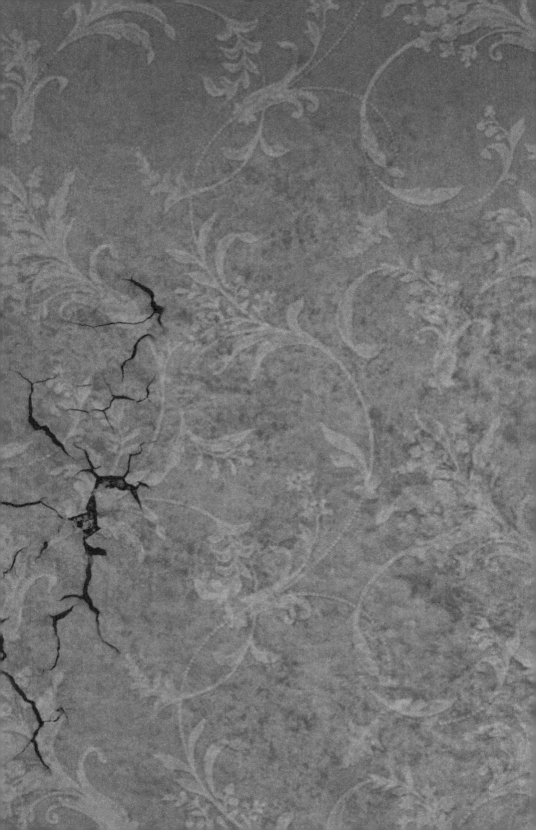

Twenty-One

Unquiet sleepers

The darkness beckoned and waited. The house stood still, the eaves held their silence, the floorboards made no sound. Theodora dared to take the first step into the waiting quiet, the pitch so absolute she could see nothing at all.

There was a mustiness surrounding her, something sweet and familiar. She paused, sensing Cassias close behind her, the same scent of cobweb and syrup clinging to every part of him. Not unpleasant, but unusual. She could not place what that strange smell reminded her of. It was all around them, woven into the darkness. Another step and the smell thickened, and she knew it then. It had wrapped around the woodwork at Broken Oak, seeped through the layers of old petticoats and silk. It was bent feathers and milky eyes, a viewing room of someone departed, the lingering musk that crept around her grandmother. The scent of lost things, of grief.

She felt her way into the pitch, fingers closing over the thick velvet of an old curtain, the fabric clinging to a circular window.

"Theodora…"

With a quick pull, she loosened the swathe of moth-eaten velvet from its railing, allowing it to fall and gather at their feet. Moonlight rushed through the dirt-glazed window, catching on webs and years of dust and abandonment.

And there it fell, that filmy streak of light, onto the secret the house did not wish to tell. The truth shattered open with a howl, an agonized cry Theodora knew that, no matter the wishing, no matter the longing to fold back into the darkness, would never quiet.

Where is your wife, Cassias Thorne?

The lord of Broken Oak Manor stepped closer, hands at his mouth as if to catch the awful noise coming from it. Another step and he fell to his knees, reaching across the dust-streaked floorboards to grasp the withered hand of Ottoline Thorne.

I cannot hear her, I cannot find her...

Theodora swallowed her own cry, forcing it down to smother her racing heart. She stared, willing the desolation before her to change, to be a trick of the light—to be a dream and nothing more. But Cassias's screams carried on, wretched and real.

The remains in pink frill and lace sat huddled against a desiccated husk shrouded in the graying remains of a dress shirt. The ruby pinned at its neck gleamed softly in the dirty moonlight, like a bead of blood against the tattered silk.

"Stop screaming." The words hissed through her gritted teeth. "Stop it." Theodora pressed a hand against the ache in her chest, feeling for the steadying beat of her heart. "Stop!"

She fled the room, the dreadful howls chasing her down the hallway, into the darkness. Down and down she ran, feet frantic but soundless on the winding stairs—still the echoes followed her, filling the very air with the sound of distress, of sorrow. It echoed off the walls, that terrible howl, seeping into the woodwork, until the silent house was silent no more.

She ran into the foyer, the shards of broken glass dusting the floor twinkling under the moonlight, forgotten. She paused for a moment, gathering her wits, her sensibilities. Her thoughts were scattered, as fragmented as the glass beneath her feet. Gathering her skirts, Theodora made to flee Broken Oak, flee the monstrosity in the attic, and found herself running straight into Ms. Rivers.

Theodora's knees buckled, but the housekeeper's firm grip upon her arms kept her from sinking to the floor. Her bony fingers dug into Theodora's arms, firm and unyielding, lips set in a thin, cold line.

"I told you not to go into the attic, Miss Corvus," she began, looking toward the sound of the screaming. "I told you to have a care."

Theodora tore herself away, sprawling upon the hard floor. "You knew! You knew what lay hidden within this house, beneath its eaves. You knew and allowed us to carry on with that...that *desecration* above us."

"And what would you have had me do, Miss Corvus?" She kept one hand against Theodora's arm, her grip softening, fingers almost gentle. "Is Cassias happier for the knowing, I wonder? Are you?"

The cries from the attic grew quieter, becoming rasps, breathless and raw. Theodora wished he would scream instead.

"Then you should have done something, Ms. Rivers," she said, desperate. "You cannot just leave them up there!"

"What am I to do, Theodora?" The housekeeper's voice was softer than she had ever heard it. A caress of words. "I cannot leave this house."

Theodora pulled her arm away, cradling it against her chest. "Don't be absurd."

Ms. Rivers smiled, reaching out to tenderly touch the exposed beams above her. "I do so love making tea, Miss Corvus. I can almost smell it, the lemon and the bergamot, there are times where I believe I can truly smell it. The candles and fireplaces took time to master, I will admit. So long, that I can't quite remember when first I learned..."

"I have seen you crochet," Theodora hissed, stepping back, stepping away.

187

The old housekeeper nodded, pulling her hook and square of crochet from her apron pocket. "You would think it would grow tiresome, after all this time—spending hours on a beloved craft, never able to finish."

"You are mocking me!" Theodora exclaimed. "If this is a hideous prank..."

"People see what they wish to see, Miss Corvus," the housekeeper replied, placing the unfinished crochet back into her pocket. "And our minds fill in the gaps."

"Nonsense," the word hissed from Theodora's lips, but she looked to the ceiling above. "All this time...they have been up there, all this time?"

"For a while," came the reply, soft and awful.

Theodora lifted her chin, voice scornful. "And you, Ms. Rivers?"

"I remember not, girl. I have always been here, seen by many and unseen by most." Ms. Rivers gave a small smile, eyes hard and cold. "I neither ask the why behind it, nor do I care for the answer. I just am and I am content with that."

The hallway grew quiet, the sounds from the attic slipping further into the walls of the house. It drank them in, like oil on parched wood.

"I warned you away from the attic, girl," Ms. Rivers said, arms folded. "What good do you think you have done, showing him?"

"This is madness." Theodora backed away, hands against the wall. "You are all mad!"

"Where is his wife, Miss Corvus? Where is Eleanor Thorne?" Ms. Rivers tilted her head, waiting.

Theodora thought of the wisps of white skirts, the ruined painting, the broken glass and tormented cries. The wails of a guilt-ridden soul.

One of flesh and blood.

"May you all be damned!" she spat, ready to tear away from Broken Oak with its dreadful secrets and wandering souls. Not wanting to hear more, Theodora ran, Ms. Rivers's call chasing at her heels.

"How far will you get, Theodora Corvus, in your damp skirts and muddied shoes?"

~

The looming shadow of Broken Oak Manor stretched across the lawns, lit by the moonlight, lit by the flickering candles resting upon the windowsills. Theodora willed herself on, to not look back, not care or think—fearing the weight of it all crushing her. And it would, that weight, that grief—it would calcify around her heart and pull her under.

She found the road not too far from the woods surrounding Broken Oak. She remembered it well, the tired and bruised walk along the stones and weeds. She remembered the relief she felt when Broken Oak had come into view, how the feeling of desperation to leave it behind now drowned that out. Those memories she had made beneath its roof were stained, as ruined as the secret that lay within its attic.

Mist coiled from the lake ahead, thick and cold. No watchers lingered by the water. The mist curled around her, pulled at her skirts.

"Miss Corvus?"

She spun, not having noticed the approach of Ottoline Thorne.

"Away with you!"

The girl remained where she stood, pale hand outstretched. "Come back to the house."

"Leave me be, Ottoline," Theodora whispered, pleading. "I only wish to go home."

"You will not leave here, Miss Corvus," Ottoline said, her voice soft and quiet and terrible.

"You knew also, didn't you?" Theodora pointed a finger at the young girl, wishing to remove the image of her in rotting silk from her mind. "All this time I spent with you, and you knew."

"I remember," Ottoline said with a wistful smile. "Like Ms. Rivers recalls the taste of Earl Grey, I remember the bitter taste of poison, and that it was only meant for me. She did not expect Papa to take tea with me that day. I wanted her to like me, Miss Corvus, for Papa's sake, I wanted to see him happy again. She scorned me from the moment she set eyes on me, all in secret, of course, when no one was looking. She would give me gifts, dolls and paints and bows for my hair, but she wouldn't give me her heart. There was no room set aside for me there. I didn't fit."

Theodora stepped closer, unable to turn her back on the girl she had allowed into her tear-hardened heart. "I don't understand."

Ottoline shrugged, a subtle lift to her shoulder as though it all meant little to her. "Lady Thorne wanted an heir of her own; it is that simple."

"She was at the house today..."

Ottoline wrapped her arms around her little body, daring a glance over her shoulder. "She never left, Miss Corvus."

Theodora followed her gaze, through the darkness, to where she knew Broken Oak Manor stood watch. "I would know if she was living in the house, Ottoline."

A smile lifted the edge of the child's rosebud lips. It was not a kind smile, not a good smile. "If you say so, Miss Corvus." Ottoline placed a hand to her mouth, concealing her grin, and leaned closer. "She does not like it when we move things."

"You are frightening me, Ottoline, stop."

Closer she stepped, soundless. "Come home with me. Papa will miss you."

"I will not go back to that house!" Theodora hissed. "I will go home to my grandmother."

"You cannot leave here, Miss Corvus."

Theodora longed for Woodrow House, for the creaking beams

and crumbling walls and the sound of her grandmother, her voice, the croak of her lungs. "Why can't I?"

Ottoline lifted a pale hand. "Your skirts are wet."

The mist had soaked through her clothing, heavy and cold. "Go home, Ottoline, find your peace within that house and allow me to find mine within Woodrow's walls. I do not belong here."

"Can you not see, Miss Corvus?" Ottoline drew closer, small hand reaching out to interlock with hers. "When was the last time your skirts felt dry, truly dry? When did you last sit down for tea? Oh, Miss Corvus, when was the last time a morsel of food slipped past your lips?"

The house was quiet; it had not spoken to her as other houses had. It had waited and listened, drawing in terrible secrets not for Theodora to hear. No watchers stood at the water's edge at Broken Oak. No one had waited.

But Theodora had waited.

"I thought of a name for you," Theodora began, whisper soft, her feet rooted to the ground beneath. "In that house, up in that room, under everything...it came to me."

"What would you call me, Miss Corvus?"

Theodora settled her gaze on Ottoline, at the girl that spring would never touch, whose wishes would remain, as she would remain, locked away and unfulfilled. "Little Wren, Ottoline. I would call you Little Wren."

With her hand tight in Ottoline's, Theodora scaled down the embankment, feet silent. Still silent. Always silent. The wheel tracks were long erased by the rain and wind, but Theodora knew where to look. And look, she did.

There it lay, near-hidden by storm-loosened branches, the dark waters almost claiming it completely. Her carriage, overturned and broken. The horses lay beneath it, shattered and ruined. The driver, still clinging to his whip, lay hunched over and pinned by one unfor-giving bough. He did not watch. He had not waited.

Slowly, ever so slowly, she waded to the carriage, the water rising past her waist, her chest, her neck. And she felt nothing at all. She went to the door, feet skimming the coarse grit, and there, with a quiet calmness, she peered through the window.

No wail broke from Theodora's lips, no scream or cry. She stood quite silent, a hand firm to her chest, as if to feel for the heart beneath her fingertips. She felt its weight, the hardness of it, the fullness of it. It was there, beneath her ribs, tear-soaked and love-swollen, and she bent over, nails digging in as though to claw it from her breast.

Theodora Corvus stared back at herself through the window, river-drowned and bloated. Eye sockets empty, lips black, lungs too full and heart not full enough.

"Come," Ottoline said gently. "Come home, Miss Corvus."

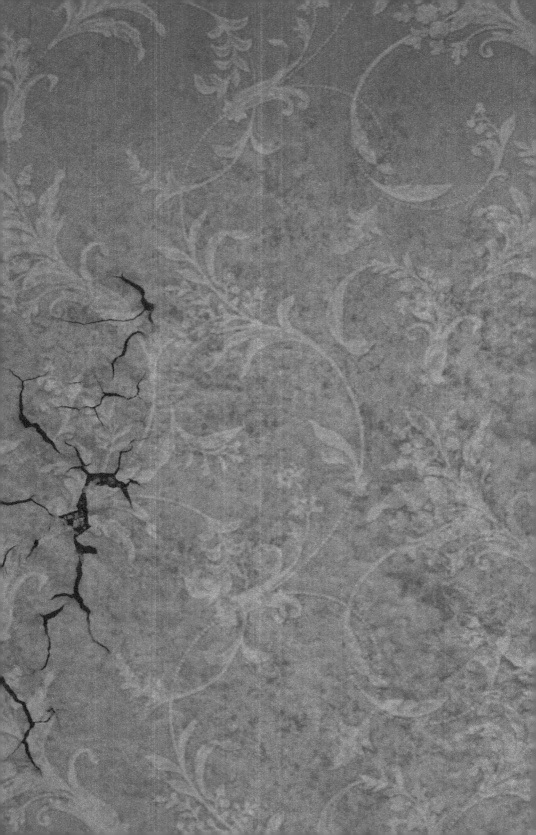

Twenty-Two

Less the depth of grief

Broken Oak stood in shadow, whisper-quiet and waiting. Ottoline's hand remained folded over her own, and they felt solid, real—as they always had. They returned to Broken Oak without a word; there was no more to be said. The walk back settled Theodora's bones, drawing her closer. It was a strange sensation— one of weightlessness yet, at the same time, as though a thread hung at her center, pulling her in.

Pulling her home.

Moonlight draped over the edges of the manor, softening the darkness. Gentle light slipped across the grass, tangling in the bare branches, casting a silvery glow upon all it touched. It fell upon a waiting Cassias, standing tall and silent.

"Papa!" Ottoline broke free of her hold and ran toward the doorway, feet soundless, always soundless, straight into her father's arms. Theodora followed, slower, the weight of her heart making no mark upon the ground she walked.

Cassias held his daughter close, head buried in her soft hair. Theodora wondered if he could still smell the soap on her, the scent of childhood, of flesh and blood. Or if, like Cassias himself, she took on the scent of the attic—all cobwebs and slow decay.

He was weeping; she could see that. Not the wild, agonized sobs she had fled, but quiet tears full of sorrow and loss. Theodora touched her own cheek, feeling the wetness of her own tears. They were as real as she, her very soul weeping.

From the doorway, from the darkness, Ms. Rivers stepped out and leaned against the wall, arms folded. She took in the sight of Theodora and gave her a small nod. It was a gesture of acknowledgement, of understanding. There would be no comforting words from the housekeeper, no coddling. For that, Theodora's fondness for the old woman increased.

Ottoline whispered to her father, and he set her back down, hands reluctant to let her go. With a gentle squeeze she pulled away, and walked back into the house with Ms. Rivers.

They were left alone, looking at each other and, in silence, beneath the stretching shadows, they moved closer. Cassias reached out first, hand stopping a breath away from Theodora.

"I am so sorry," he said, not touching her, so close yet not close enough.

Theodora stepped into him, feeling the firmness of his body, the warmth of his hands. If they were but stardust and memory, then it mattered little.

"This is not your doing, Cassias Thorne," she whispered, drawing him close. "If this is to be my adventure, then so be it." She sighed against him, allowing the weight of it all to settle around her —yet it did not pull her down. It hung, more like an anchor; a strange feeling that she was where she was meant to be. "I can think of worse fates than staying by your side as eternity slips by."

"We will never leave here." He turned to the house, gleaming in moonlight with its secrets spilled. "I wanted so much to leave this place."

"Death comes to all of us in the end," Theodora said, more to herself. "We don't get to choose it."

"I would have hoped for a better one," Cassias replied. "I hoped for a far distant one for Ottoline."

She rested against him, head on his shoulder, his embrace firm and soft all at once. "I have no words of comfort for you."

"And I none for you, Theodora." He sighed, lips finding the hollow of her neck. He lay sweet, gentle kisses on her skin. "I would not choose this death, but I did not want the life I had either. But this—" He kissed her again, reaching into hair. "This..."

Her mouth found his, her words slipping past. "This, Cassias, we journey through together."

∼

With the moonlight a beacon above her, Theodora stepped out over the lawns of Broken Oak, skirts trailing around her, hemline damp and muddied as they had been for some time. Cassias walked beside her, a quiet companion, his hand in hers. Together they wandered to the edge of the pond, the waters still as glass.

Theodora gazed out over the water, to the other side where the reeds grew taller, and there she stayed, in silence, chin up and back straight.

Come and find me, come and wait with me. She sent those wishes, as silent as the waters, into the space between her heart and her hope and she felt the weight of them. She felt the weight of Ottoline's wishes also, boxed up with no place to go.

Ottoline had known, with every wish she had written, that they would not come to pass, that they would stay locked within the music box as reminders of what could have been, what would have been, if the world was a kinder place. The sorrow of those wishes ached, made heavier in the knowing there was so little hope behind them. Ottoline would never see the seaside, ride the donkeys on the promenade, hear the music of the carousel calliope. She would never leave Broken Oak; and she had known, and still she had wished.

No one else stood beneath the shadows of the winter-bare trees, not the mother she did not know, nor the father she had known for too little. They were not there, and Theodora understood they had no reason to be, yet still she longed for them. Reasoning had no place in her grief. It was a thought unbearable to fathom, that wherever her parents went, if their souls existed at all, that Theodora could never follow.

"Who is it you search for?" Cassias asked, voice slipping through the quiet, his presence grounding. "At the water's edge?"

Theodora did not turn away from the pond, but her fingers tightened over his, and answered both for him and herself. "For those I know will never come."

"Did you..." he paused, voice faltering. "Did you see...did anyone ever wait for you, at Woodrow?"

She faced him then, his eyes downcast as though to search for the words that had tumbled so clumsily from his lips. "Never anyone I knew," she answered, voice soft. "None that brought comfort to me."

"I saw them at times," Cassias said, eyes flicking to hers. "Here at Broken Oak, by the pond, by the water. I would look for her...for Rose, knowing that if she could linger, could wait for me, she would. She would have waited for me."

Theodora looked back out to the water's edge, to the emptiness that greeted her. "Where did they go, those black-eyed watchers?"

Cassias said nothing for a time, and then with a breath and a tightening of his hand he whispered, "I am not sure they went anywhere, Theodora."

She peered through the shadows, the moonlit reeds and the barren branches, and still saw nothing. She remembered the black eyes of those that stood by the lake at Woodrow, the way they would turn to her, ever silent. She remembered their smiles, their mirthless grins and the way they waited and waited and waited.

Waited for what?

Salvation

"We are not like them," Theodora said, stepping away from the water. Cassias stepped back also, hand remaining in hers. "We need no saving. You and I and Ms. Rivers and dear little Ottoline seek no salvation within this world, nor beyond it. We are not damned."

"Are we merely stuck, then, Theodora? Set to linger in this half-life for all eternity?" Cassias swept a hand out, gesturing to the moon-drenched lawns, to the looming shadow of Broken Oak standing tall and silent upon its hill. "To what end?"

"Am I to answer that, Cassias?" she replied, knowing she sought such answers too, and knowing they likely would never come. "I do not know the reasoning of it, only that I have no say on the matter. Do you remain because you longed to raise your daughter? As I remain because I longed for more? Ottoline is tied to you, the threads of whatever we are...the souls we may be are knotted tight, so surely, they will never come apart." She took a breath, feeling it deep in her chest and realizing the absurdity of it all. "And Ms. Rivers..."

"Ms. Rivers remains because of her infernal never-ending crochet."

A startled laugh slipped from Theodora, the ache at her chest easing just the smallest amount. "You jest now?"

"I feel I must, and I make no apology for it. The weight of melancholy is one I cannot bear at present. I can feel it tugging at me, waiting to pull me under." Cassias drew her closer, tucking her head beneath his chin. She fit there quite perfectly.

"I wonder if it will get easier," Theodora said, resting against the solidness of Cassias. "If we will become like Ms. Rivers and will be content in the way of things. We may grow bored, Cassias, if truly we are to be here forever."

She felt him place a kiss on the top of her head, the gesture sweet and loving. "I think it is good to be bored sometimes, to stay still, to watch the world pass by. Though, I know in my heart I will never grow bored of you."

"Not even of my teasing?"

"Not even that," He sighed, holding her closer as though afraid she would float away. "Is it awful to say that I am thankful you are here, Theodora?"

"I am here, Cassias," she said. "Awful or not, I am here."

They remained for some time at the edge of the pond, beneath the moonlight and beneath the gazes of the watchers they could no longer see. Theodora kept her head resting against Cassias, hands locked in his, sharing the weight of their grief, their loss and everything in between.

She closed her eyes, drawing forth the lasting memories of her father. The way he danced with her, the sound of his laughter, deep and wonderful. To memory she committed the smell of him, the smell of her childhood, and then she put away the dreams he had held for her that would always remain dreams, and nothing more.

For the mother she never knew, she placed the memories of her portraits beside the tear-dampened tales her father had recalled. She conjured up, from memory and dreams, an idea of her mother, one perhaps she would have been, if given the chance. She imagined the sound she could have made when she sang, a smile she wore only for her, the whispered hopes and secrets a mother kept for her daughter. It was not a real memory, not a whole one, but to Theodora it mattered not.

And for her grandmother, she tucked everything into her weighted heart until she was sure it would burst. The milk white of her eyes, the wrinkled smile, seldom and earned, the crackle of her voice, little more than an echo in her mind. Along with the memories of Woodrow, the rot and the ruin and the comfort of home, Theodora kept it all. Kept it all tight within herself, into the space where the grief had once settled. She made room for it, those memories and she did not lock it tight, and when the time was right and she was ready, she would share it all.

With one last glance at the water, Theodora walked away, hand in hand with Cassias Thorne. Although she knew she would come to the pond often, to paint, to picnic, to watch spring touch the edges of Broken Oak, she would no longer search the shadows. She would no longer seek out the faces of her family, they were not there. They had not waited, and for that Theodora was thankful.

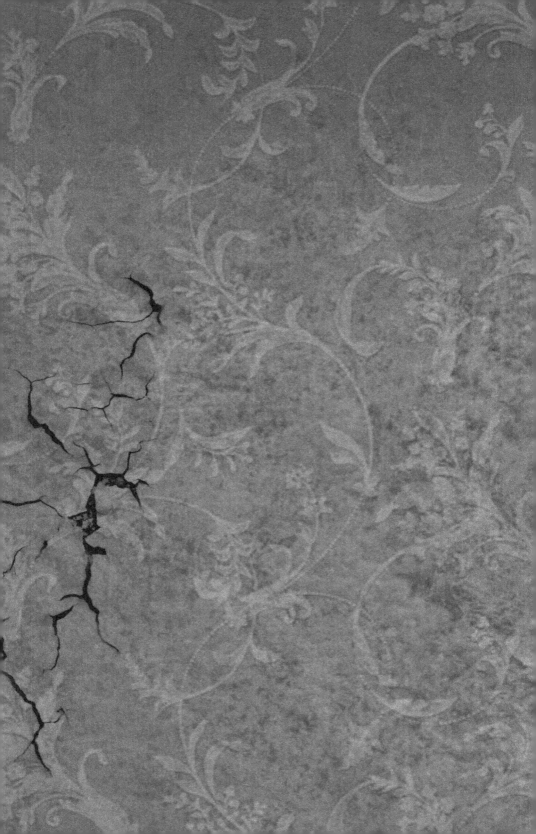

Twenty-Three

All my heart is yours

Time stopped and slipped by, slowing and changing with a will of its own. Cassias no longer sleepwalked, no longer wandered the darkened halls of Broken Oak seeking answers for questions he had not asked. A quiet sort of peace settled over him, his dark eyes becoming brighter, his smile finding his lips with greater ease.

Theodora found that, for the first time in so very long, her skirts were dry, the hemline darker than the rest of her skirts, but the dampness gone. The chill that had seeped into her bones was also gone and she felt warm. She felt the warmth of Cassias, the touch of his hand on hers, the softness of his kiss, his love, and everything in between. The weight she carried within her breast still remained, as she had no doubts it always would, yet she found she could bear it with a new ease. It was a comfort to her, to be weighed down by the love she carried for those she had lost. And between them, with their hands entwined and souls tangled, the weight of grief was lighter still.

Theodora continued Ottoline's lessons, knowing it did little good to grow idle. With the mischievous glint in the young girl's eyes growing brighter each day, Theodora surmised that boredom would only lead to mayhem, and she had little patience for silliness. So Ottoline continued to paint poor depictions of fruit, the edges bruised and darkened where no such decay could be seen. It left Theodora to wonder if that was how Ottoline saw the world, seeing beyond the fleeting glow of life to the rot beneath.

One afternoon, with the early spring sunshine trickling over the constant clouds, Theodora questioned Ottoline. They had moved onto portraits, and she had painted Theodora with steely concentration, tight lipped and serious. Theodora had sat with patience, no words between them, just the soft sounds of the paint-soaked brush flowing over canvas.

Ottoline had finished with a flourish of her brush, and turned the portrait to face Theodora. She felt herself still, the breath she knew she no longer had, seeming to thicken. A coldness slipped over them, heavy and wrong.

Ottoline had painted bone and shadow.

"I do not look like that," Theodora had said, horrified, pointing to the gray shades of mottled skin, to the yellow of old bone.

Ottoline had tilted her chin, blue eyes bright and sad, "Yes, you do."

"Paint me as I am, Ottoline." She reached across the paints and the brushes to grasp Ottoline's hands. "As you see me now, Little Wren, for I am here and my bones are not."

"I can feel them, Miss Corvus, in the attic, the bones of who I was. Can you not feel your own?"

Theodora could. If she thought too long, too hard she could feel the wetness of them, the numbing cold, the unmoving finality of it all. "They say if you lose a limb, you can still feel it there, feel it move, feel the pain of it. Is this so very different? We are severed from our earthly remains, but our memories are not."

A small smile, barely there at all, lifted the edges of Ottoline's rosebud lips. With care, she turned and picked up her paintbrush, and without looking away from Theodora, she dipped it into ink-black paint. Theodora sat and waited, watching as the paintbrush dipped into more black, drops of it slipping down the tip to splatter onto the floorboards.

At last, she revealed her new creation, the smile slipping into something akin to nervousness, though Theodora could not be entirely sure. And there it was, an inkblot of muddied black. Brush-strokes of it had been dragged over the canvas, swallowing up the bone and the shadows and all that Theodora once was, still was and would always be. Outwards the black stretched, curved lines and quick strokes, some of the paint giving way to the white of untouched canvas. She could see the suggestion of wings, of an open beak, of a bird taking flight.

Not just any bird. A jackdaw.

"I see you, Miss Corvus." Ottoline pointed to a set of smaller wings, depicted in shades of tawny brown and soft white. "As you see me."

Just like Broken Oak itself, the old housekeeper changed little, despite all the secrets the house had spilled out. She continued her never ending crochet and brewed pots of fragrant tea no one would ever drink. She lit the fireplaces and the candles and kept the floors clean as she always had done, and seemed always would. She was a part of the house, made up of memory and stubbornness.

She carried herself differently, however, standing straighter, as though no longer burdened with the awful secrets she had stowed away. They were not hers to let loose, she had told Theodora. They had not been for Theodora to seek out, the housekeeper told her also, though sought them out she had. And Theodora had asked, with great curiosity, what she expected the outcome to be, that nothing remained hidden forever and the truth, as awful as it was, would eventually spill out.

To that, the housekeeper had given a sniff, lips pursed and

answered, "I have been in this house far longer than you girl, we wake up to the realization of how things are, given time. With time, Miss Corvus, and some need longer than others. I told you to have a care..."

"I did care!" Theodora had answered, voice rising, "I thought—"

"You cared too much, girl, and for that I cannot blame you." There was a pause, a sigh. An acceptance. "You belong here, Miss Corvus, in this house, with us."

Afterwards, in the time that followed, Theodora would catch Ms. Rivers smiling more often, shrewd eyes content and warm.

The air itself within Broken Oak had changed, the quietness of its halls somehow softer, the silence not one of waiting, but of contentment. Neither she nor Cassias returned to the attic, to the narrow stairs, the rotting beams and the spilled secrets behind the brass. If that room, those eaves, those shadows wished to speak to her, she cared not. And if they were to be as quiet as the rest of the house, then she had no inclination to find out. Silent or not, it mattered little.

Theodora did not return to the woods, to the storm-stretched river with its broken carriage. There waited only memories, reminders of a place she could no longer return to. The letters she had written to her grandmother were handed back, unposted and unread. No apology came from the housekeeper, no kind words, but she did draw Theodora close and held her while she wept.

She wondered when her grandmother would receive news of her fate, to be left alone to bury the remains of her granddaughter beside her beloved son. She would never know Theodora had reached Broken Oak and had become so much more than a governess. She had found love and, though her grandmother may have scoffed at that, Theodora knew her father, at least, would have been proud of her. It was with great sadness, however, for Theodora to accept she would never see her grandmother again, and that her final farewell had truly been their last. There had been no finality behind the goodbye, no thought that there never again would be greetings. But that was the way of all partings, the last ones were rarely foretold.

It was an odd feeling, being detached from one's body, and though Theodora had been detached for quite some time, the strangeness lingered. The feeling of a phantom limb...a phantom self seemed ever present, and she had to wonder if that feeling would fade, when at last her bones were taken away.

Under the quiet timbers of Broken Oak, Theodora slumbered beside Cassias, a habit they carried on, despite lacking the need. He was warm, solid, made up of everything he had ever been. They were echoes of themselves; dreams breathed real. She lay in his arms, head against his chest, the absence of a heartbeat no longer strange.

They were unlike the specters by the lake, black eyed and silent. They were not waiting—there was no one to save them. They needed no salvation.

There was no hurry to their existence, no urgency and they were the happier for it. They often watched the skies darken from the comfort of their bed, with the candlelight low, the fire dancing softly, and the stars in the endless black racing across the night. They watched sunrises and sunsets and the slow changing of seasons, often alone, held by each other. And other times with the warmth of Ottoline between them.

In the darkness, they lay tangled, drawn to each other in sleep as they had been the moment they met. It was as though their souls could see the grief they shared, the sorrow and the loneliness and had reached out, and refused to let go.

A screech tore Theodora from that deep and wonderful sleep, Cassias bolting upright beside her. They often heard the wails and screams of the living—the woman in white, whose footsteps echoed in the darkness. Theodora no longer followed the sound of footsteps, the sigh of skirts over the floorboards. No one did. They did, however, leave the candles burning in rooms Eleanor had vacated and dampened the fires in rooms where she sought warmth.

Once, Ottoline had tired of the relentless rocking in her room, and in a fit of rage had plucked her unloved doll from its resting place and tossed it at the wall, shattering the porcelain face into a thousand shards. The screams had rattled the walls of the house, and the rocking chair had remained still ever since.

Ottoline had learned to light the candles the following day, and Ms. Rivers gained a helping hand in keeping the fires they wanted lit, and the candlelight they wanted, dancing. Though Theodora still held an intolerance to pranks, she did turn a blind eye to the torment inflicted upon the lady of the house. They would often hear Eleanor weeping in the rooms above them, a mournful sound that bled no sympathy from Theodora.

Yet the scream that pulled Theodora from her dreams sounded different, angry...desperate.

"Have we finally driven her mad?" Cassias mumbled, dragging the covers higher around himself.

He spoke little of Eleanor, seeming almost indifferent to knowing she had stolen his life—as though it mattered little, that perhaps in some way he thought he had deserved no less. There was a cold fury he possessed for Ottoline, and Ottoline alone, a raw agony at her demise that threatened to buckle him. Although she was with him for always, loved and coddled as all children should be, it haunted him as much as he haunted Broken Oak. Theodora knew there was no forgiveness in him, not for Eleanor and not for the world, for the injustice of Ottoline's mayfly life.

Cassias sunk deeper into the pillows. "I do so hope she has fallen into madness."

"No...listen." Theodora hauled him upright, fingers locked with his, their bodies always tangled together. "There's someone else there."

They listened to strange voices slipping into the darkness and it coaxed them out of bed. The voices were low and many, echoing through the corridors of Broken Oak. Hand in hand, Theodora and Cassias wandered onto the landing, meeting Ottoline's sleepy face in the twilit space.

"You heard it too?" Cassias asked, looking past his daughter, to where the voices drifted up through the night.

Ottoline nodded, stepping into Theodora's waiting arms. She lifted the child against her hip, one hand around her small body, the other still claimed by her father. "Who is it? What do they want?"

"I supposed we should find out," Theodora replied, turning to Cassias.

"This house gives me so little peace." Annoyance filled Cassias's voice, rather than a weariness. "It is my house! The sheer audacity of entering another man's house without invitation."

Ms. Rivers hurried around the corner, face livid. "There is someone treading mud all over my floors! There are men here!"

"For goodness's sake." Cassias stormed down the corridor, hand still tight in Theodora's, forcing her to follow. Ottoline still rested against her hip, eyes wide and curious, lips ever so slightly turned up at her father's frustration. Ms. Rivers followed behind, arms crossed, murmuring about the state of her floors, the footprints on her rugs.

They made a strange sort of family, Theodora knew that, but together they gathered in the grand foyer, gathered on the stairs to watch.

Eleanor Thorne was screaming, back arching, fingers clawing against the hands restraining her. Chains dangled from her wrists, clashing against the wooden floor. She looked so unlike her portrait, hair unbound and wild, white skirts stained with soot from the fires she could not keep lit.

Others passed by them—men in fine suits, slower and quiet, holding white sheets between them. They were silent, heads down, hands gentle. Theodora turned Ottoline's head away and brought Cassias closer.

"I am here, Theodora," he whispered, the anger gone, voice soft, trembling only ever so slightly. "I am no longer blood and bone, but I am here."

She kissed the top of his head, loving him ever more. "And you are not alone."

They took the bones from the attic, faces grave and pale. Others came by, and Theodora noticed their wet clothing, the mud they trod over Ms. Rivers's lovely clean floors. She found herself sighing, releasing a breath long held. They had found her, also, drowned and cold but no longer lost. Those earthly remains of her, at least, would see Woodrow again.

Cassias did not turn to see them leave, to see Lady Thorne dragged from their home, her face going white, eyes wide as she locked gazes with Theodora.

Theodora Corvus grinned, and it was not a good smile, not a kind smile. Eleanor Thorne did not smile back.

Acknowledgments

There are so many people I would like to thank, and I really hope I remember them all here.

Thank you to my wonderful critique partner, Chesney Infalt, for reading a very early draft of Empty Houses and for believing I had something special.

To Stephen Black for all your support from the beginning, from the Wicked Woods to haunted houses, thank you for encouraging me to push myself, for seeking something else for Empty Houses.

I would like to give a heartfelt thank you to Cassandra and the entire team at Quill and Crow. This has been an amazing adventure; thank you for finding a home for Theodora Corvus. I couldn't wish for better.

Thank you to my editor Red, for bringing out the best in my writing, for tweaking certain phrases just so and making them sing.

Thank you Alma for all your marketing expertise! I have now taken a liking to reading aloud.

As always, a thank you to my husband Matt, for understanding my need to write and write and write. Thank you for your ongoing support and love. Love you always.

To my girls, my imps, you may not live in a haunted house, which is a terrible shame, but I hope the Ghosts of Broken Oak one day find themselves in your hands.

About the Author

L.V. Russell grew up in a haunted cottage deep in the Dorset countryside alongside her three elder brothers, using the fields and woodland as their playground. As an adult with two young children, she has used the memories of the wild woods of her youth to write stories about faeries and ghosts and the old whispering oaks. When she is not writing, she is most likely to be found exploring the woods near her home, or curled up by candlelight with a good book.

Also by L.V. Russell
Darling, There Are Wolves in the Woods
Hush, The Woods Are Darker Still
Far Beneath the Wicked Woods

Thank You For Reading

Thank you for reading The Quiet Stillness of Empty Houses. We deeply appreciate our readers, and are grateful for everyone who takes the time to leave us a review. If you're interested, please visit our website to find review links. Your reviews help small presses and indie authors thrive, and we appreciate your support.

Other Titles by Quill & Crow

Her Dark Enchantments

The Blood Bound Series

All the Parts of the Soul

The Ancient Ones Trilogy

QUILL & CROW
PUBLISHING HOUSE

CPSIA information can be obtained
at www.ICGtesting.com
Printed in the USA
JSHW020245300523
42342JS00001B/77